ro
ro
ro

ro
ro
ro

Stefanie Schulz
Daniel Quinlan

Touchdown in Amerika

Eine deutsch-englische Geschichte

Rowohlt Taschenbuch Verlag

Für H. und H.

Originalausgabe
Veröffentlicht im Rowohlt Taschenbuch Verlag,
Reinbek bei Hamburg, Januar 2010

Lektorat Christiane Steen
Umschlaggestaltung any.way, Barbara Hanke/Cordula Schmidt
(Umschlagillustration: Barbara Korthues)
Satz Minion PostScript, InDesign, bei
Pinkuin Satz und Datentechnik, Berlin
Druck und Bindung Druckerei C. H. Beck, Nördlingen
Printed in Germany
ISBN 978 3 499 21539 1

Inhalt

Kapitel eins –

The news of the year

BÄNG! Es schepperte. Der Fußball flog gegen das Garagentor. Nico nahm den Ball gekonnt mit dem Fuß auf, dribbelte ein wenig über den Asphalt und schoss dann wieder gegen das Tor. Er holte mit voller Wucht aus, und der Ball prallte hart und laut an der Garage ab. Doch keiner der Nachbarn wunderte sich oder schaute erschreckt aus dem Fenster. Alle Bewohner des Schäferwegs waren schon daran gewöhnt, dass es nachmittags rummste und krachte. Denn der 15-jährige Nico Wagner kickte schon solange alle denken konnten jeden Nachmittag vor dem Haus seiner Eltern mit seinem schon ziemlich abgenutzten Lederfußball. Ruhe hatte die Nachbarschaft nur, wenn er sich mit seinem Ball auf eine der angrenzenden Wiesen verzog, um dort mit seinen Kumpels aus der Schule zu spielen. Bei schlechtem Wetter trafen sie sich bei einem von ihnen zu Hause und probten ihr Kicker-Können am Computer. Und dann war da natürlich noch das Training im Verein jeden Montag-, Mittwoch- und Freitagabend …

Nico konnte sich einfach nichts Besseres vorstellen als Fußball, Fußball und nochmal Fußball! Es gab einfach keinen Zweifel: Fußball war die beste Sache der Welt!

Nico war so in Gedanken versunken, dass er einige Sekunden brauchte, um das Geräusch zu bemerken, das zu den «Bängs» und «Rrrummms» seines Fußballs hinzugekommen war. Es war die Klingel am Fahrrad des Postboten. Erst vor ein paar Wochen hatte Nico den Postboten fast umgerannt, als er hinter einem Ball hergehechtet war. Seitdem kündigte der sich lieber aus sicherer Entfernung an. Als Nico den Briefträger bemerkt hatte, hielt er den Ball mit dem Fuß fest und grinste. Der Postbote stellte sein Rad ab, ging zum Briefkasten der Wagners und steckte einen dicken Stapel Briefe hinein. Einen großen, prallgefüllten Umschlag behielt er aber in der Hand. Er kam damit auf Nico zu und rief: «Heute ist etwas für dich dabei!» Er übergab Nico den Umschlag, setzte sich auf sein Rad und fuhr zum nächsten Haus.

Nico war überrascht. Normalerweise gab es nie Post für ihn! Okay, letzten Monat war mal eine Mahnung von der Schulbibliothek gekommen – aber so einen dicken Umschlag hatte er noch nie bekommen. Dann entdeckte er auf der Vorderseite einen kleinen Aufkleber mit dem Schriftzug «by air mail». Das war doch nicht etwa …?! Nico merkte, wie sein Puls in die Höhe schoss, als hätte er gerade einen Sprint hingelegt. Er drehte den Umschlag um und las den Absender: International Student Exchange Office, USA.

On the same day in Charlotte, North Carolina, Kimberly Williams was standing high up on the bleachers of her high school's football field. Although it was still early in the morning, the sun was up and shining brightly into her eyes. Kimmy, as all her friends called her, was wearing a pair of denim shorts, a green t-shirt and green flip-flops. Her long black braided hair fell over her dark brown shoulders as she leaned forward to take her sunglasses out of her purse. She put them on, sat down and yawned. She had gotten up extra early, and she was still tired. Really tired.

Kimmy looked around sleepily. The bleachers where the fans usually sat were empty, and the vast football field lay in front of her deserted, too. She was completely alone. It was nearly silent, except for the sound of some morning insects. Kimmy rested her legs on the seat in front of her, stroked her hair out of her face and made herself comfortable. The quiet morning gently invited her back to sleep. Kimmy relaxed and closed her eyes.

Suddenly, without warning, loud hip-hop music blasted from the field's loudspeakers. Kimmy jumped from her seat. A group of girls came running onto the field, chanting a school cheer to the beat of the music. Kimmy remembered immediately why she had come to the football field. She sighed, took a notebook and a pencil out of her bag and sat down again. «Wake up, Kimmy,» she told herself, «you're here to work!» She thought for a second, and then wrote:

Summer Workout: Jeff High Cheerleaders better than ever!

«Kimmy! Hey!» somebody shouted. Kimmy looked up and saw her best friend, Ashley McMannon, standing in front of her. Ashley was wearing the Jefferson High School cheerleader uniform: a short red skirt with a sleeveless red, white and blue top. Her long blonde hair was pulled back into a ponytail.

«Hey Ashley,» she greeted her friend. «What are you doing up here? Shouldn't you be on the field with the other cheerleaders?»

«Yeah,» Ashley nodded. «… but I saw you and I came over to say hi … what are you doing here anyway?»

«I'm here for the Express, remember?» Kimmy said. «I'm doing the article about the cheerleading squad's summer workout, how you already started practicing before the school year begins.»

«Oh, right, the school newspaper. ‹The Express!›» Ashley said and giggled a little at herself. «I always forget all these things about school during the summer. How's the newspaper doing?»

Kimmy smiled. «Well, we have a really good team working on the Express. I think it's going to be a good year for us.»

«Totally!» Ashley grinned. «I mean, now that you're the Express star reporter!»

«I don't know about all that,» Kimmy answered, trying to be modest. «But you know, I do really love this job! It's so much fun to write and to interview people and to take photos …»

«Totally, I know what you mean …» Ashley said and looked back towards her fellow cheerleaders, who looked like they were about to practice one of their organized routines. «Looks like I have to go.» She pointed her thumb towards the field and her teammates. Then, her eyes lit up as she remembered something. «Oh, there's another thing I wanted to tell you! But then, since you are the star reporter,» she grimaced, «you probably already heard the big news!»

«What news?» Kimmy asked.

Nico riss den Umschlag auf. Seine Hände zitterteren, so nervös war er plötzlich. Ein paar Prospekte und etwas, das aussah wie eine Landkarte, fielen auf den Boden, doch er kümmerte sich gar nicht darum. Hastig faltete er den Brief auseinander und begann zu lesen.

> Dear Nicolas,
> Congratulations! You have been accepted to our German-American exchange program. Your host family, the McMannons from Charlotte, NC, are looking forward to meeting you. School starts on August 31st. We recommend that you arrive in Charlotte a few days earlier. Once you have bought tickets, please contact our office by e-mail so that we can arrange for you to be picked you up from the airport. Your host family's details have been enclosed with this letter. Please get in touch with them right away so that you can get to know them before you arrive.

Da war noch irgendeine Unterschrift unter dem Brief, doch dafür reichte Nicos Geduld nicht mehr. Schnell klaubte er die Zettel vom Boden auf, kickte den Fußball, der ihn plötzlich gar nicht mehr interessierte, aus dem Weg und rannte ins Haus.

«Mam!» Im Wohnzimmer war seine Mutter nicht. Aufgeregt lief er weiter. Auch in der Küche war niemand.

Nico rannte die Treppe hinauf. «Maaaaam!»

Er riss die Tür des Arbeitszimmers auf, das direkt neben der Treppe lag. Verwundert sah Frau Wagner vom Schreibtisch auf.

«Mama, guck dir das an! Ich wurde genommen. Es hat wirklich geklappt!», sprudelte es aus Nico heraus.

«Was ist los? Was soll ich mir angucken? Und was hat geklappt?» Frau Wagner war so in den Artikel, den sie gerade verfasste, vertieft, dass sie kaum etwas von seinen Worten verstanden hatte.

«Na, das Austauschprogramm – Amerika! Ich gehe für ein halbes Jahr nach Amerika!»

Jetzt hatte Nico die volle Aufmerksamkeit seiner Mutter.

Sie studierte den Brief, den Nico ihr auf den Schreibtisch geworfen hatte. «Mein Gott, im August soll das losgehen? Wir haben doch schon Ende Juli!»

«Ich kann schon fast meine Koffer packen», freute sich Nico. Einen Moment sah Frau Wagner ihren Sohn ernst an. Doch dann lächelte sie.

«Das wird ganz schön seltsam für Papa und mich», sagte sie und nahm ihren Sohn in den Arm. «Aber ich freue mich für dich. Das ist so eine tolle Chance. Wenn ich damals in deinem Alter diese Möglichkeit gehabt hätte, ich wäre auch sofort …»

«Ja ja», unterbrach Nico ihren Redefluss grinsend und befreite sich aus ihrer Umarmung. Vor lauter Aufregung konnte er einfach keine Sekunde länger zuhören.

Frau Wagner lachte. «Na los», sagte sie, «wolltest du nicht packen?»

«The big news! As you newspaper people say, the story of the week,» Ashley said and rolled her eyes. «Or, as I prefer to call it, the horror story of the year!»

«Come on, Ash,» Kimmy said, «what is it?»

«You know how my parents are totally weird? Like, they always have these strange ideas?» Ashley said.

«Mmh,» Kimmy nodded.

«Like last summer, when my Dad wanted us all to go to Asia to learn about martial arts, judo, karate and so on? Or when my Mom thought the whole family should spend a summer in France to study French culture? So lame! Or that one time when …» Ashley began what Kimmy knew was going to be a long list of slightly crazy ideas Mrs and Mr McMannon had had for their family.

«What is the news, Ash?» Kimmy interrupted her.

Ashley shook her head. «You know, since my parents have always wanted our family to be more … what do they call it? … more … international …» Ashley paused.

Kimmy only looked at her best friend.

«Zach and I are getting a host brother!» Ashley finally blurted out. «This boy from Germany is going to live with us for six months. He's going to go to Jeff High with us, too.»

«Wow!» Kimmy was impressed. «That actually sounds … cool!»

«I don't think it's cool *at all*! Who needs a host brother? Plus, I don't speak any ‹*Doitch*›. Njet! That's the only word I know in German,» Ashley grumbled.

«That's Russian, Ashley. ‹Njet› is Russian for ‹no›.» Kimmy laughed a little.

«See? I'm hopeless.» Ashley had to laugh now, too. «And, if you ask me …» Ashley added, «… one brother is more than enough!»

Kimmy knew that Ashley and her brother, Zach, didn't get along well. Like Ashley, he was really into sports: Ashley loved cheerleading, and Zach loved football.

But unlike his sister, who always talked a lot when Kimmy was around, Zach never said much at all. Somehow, Ashley and Zach always managed to get into fights. Kimmy didn't really understand why, and she always tried to make peace between the two.

«Zach's not that bad,» Kimmy said, «he's just … the silent type.»

«You call it silent, I call it stupid,» Ashley snapped.

«And you are pretty snappy, Ashley, and you know it,» Kimmy said with a smile.

Ashley took this as a compliment. «What's wrong with snappy?» she laughed. «At least I'm not stupid. Or boring – like my brother!»

«Well,» Kimmy said, «if this German boy moves in with you, Zach will have a new brother, too! I bet the boys will be best friends, and you won't have to deal with either of them. They'll totally leave you alone, I'm sure of it.»

«That,» Ashley said, making big, happy eyes, «is *such* a great point. One old brother plus one new brother equals no brothers at all! And if they get on my nerves – I can ignore two boys just as easily as I can one,» she joked.

Kimmy laughed.

«Oh! I really have to go now,» Ashley said and started to skip down the stairs towards the other cheerleaders. «Are you coming to my house later?»

«Of course,» Kimmy waved at her friend and took up her notebook again. «I'll see you in a few hours!»

«Give me a J-E-dou-ble-F! What does that spell? JEFF!» the girls in the red and white uniforms were now shouting as they bounced their way out onto the field.

Kimmy smiled to herself as she wrote down the first words to her article into her notebook. The Jefferson High cheerleaders were fantastic – and this was going to be a fantastic article.

Chapter Two – **Noch mehr Post**

Normalerweise benutzte Nico den PC, der auf seinem Schreibtisch stand, fast nur zum Computerspielen. Eigentlich schrieb er nicht besonders gerne E-Mails, aber jetzt wartete er ungeduldig darauf, dass sich sein E-Mail-Postfach öffnete. Es waren erst ein paar Stunden vergangen, seit Nico den Brief aus den USA erhalten hatte, aber er wollte sich auf jeden Fall noch heute bei seinen Gasteltern melden. Wie hieß die Familie nochmal? Nico schaute auf den Brief. McMannon. Komischer Name. Und wo wohnten sie genau? Charlotte, NC, stand da. Von einer Stadt namens Charlotte hatte er noch nie etwas gehört. Und was bedeuteten diese beiden Buchstaben?

Hoffentlich ist Charlotte nicht so ein klitzekleines Kuhdorf!, dachte er und öffnete ein zweites Fenster auf seinem Bildschirm. Er tippte ‹Charlotte, NC› in die Suchmaschine und klickte auf den erstbesten Link in der Liste, die auf dem Monitor erschienen war. Die Seite öffnete sich, und Nico sah sofort, dass er sich keine Sorgen machen musste, in einem kleinen Dorf zu landen: Fotos von Wolkenkratzern, breiten Straßen voller Straßenkreuzern und einem riesigen Flugplatz waren hier abgebildet, und ganz oben auf der Seite stand:

```
Welcome to Charlotte, NC!
Charlotte is the largest city in North Carolina
and the 19th largest city in the United States of
America.
```

Wow!, dachte Nico. Den Namen der Stadt fand er zwar immer noch seltsam, aber ansonsten sah das hier ziemlich gut aus. Und was das NC hinter dem Namen bedeutete, wusste er jetzt auch: North Carolina. Auf einer Landkarte, die auch auf der Webseite abgebildet war, fand er North Carolina nach kurzem Suchen: Im Südosten der Vereinigten Staaten lag das, ein ganzes Stück unterhalb von Washington, der Hauptstadt der USA, und etwas weiter nördlich als Florida.

Als Nächstes tippte Nico den Namen der Schule ein. Auch die Jefferson High School hatte natürlich eine Webseite. ‹Quick info about Jefferson High› war dort gleich der erste Link. Genau das, was ich suche, dachte Nico, öffnete das Fenster und klickte kurzerhand auf ‹drucken›, denn den Text wollte er später auch noch seinen Eltern zeigen.

Jefferson High School. Founded in 1972, named after the third president of the United States, Thomas Jefferson. Located in the South of Charlotte, NC, Jefferson High School serves several Charlotte neighborhoods and suburbs. With roughly 4000 students, it is the largest high school in the Charlotte area. Extracurricular activities include, among others, Football, Cheerleading, Student Government, Swimming and Chess. Principal: Richard D. Monroe. The following are the percentages of students in each ethnic group:
48% African American
44% Caucasian
5% Hispanic
3% Asian American
0% International

Das mit den null Prozent internationalen Schülern ändert sich dann wohl bald, grinste Nico. Auch ansonsten war dieser Text ja ganz aufschlussreich. Besonders begeistert war er natürlich, das Wort ‹Football› zu entdecken. Das fing ja schon mal gut an!

In Gedanken malte er sich aus, wie er mit seinen neuen amerikanischen Freunden – der kompletten Fußballmannschaft der Jefferson High School, natürlich – seine Freizeit verbringen würde: Er und die Jungs würden kicken und über Fußball reden! Sicherlich gab es auch ständig Spiele im Fernsehen, die sie zusammen gucken könnten …

Ansonsten fiel ihm noch auf, dass die Schule einfach riesig zu sein schien. Er erinnerte sich aus dem Englischunterricht daran, dass amerikanische High Schools nur die Klassen 9 bis 12 umfassten. Das bedeutete bei 4000 Schülern, dass jeder Jahrgang aus 1000 Leuten bestand! Unglaublich!

Viele andere Begriffe von der Website kannte Nico nicht, oder sie waren ihm zumindest nicht so ganz klar. Deswegen holte er sein Wörterbuch aus dem Regal und schlug nach. Die wichtigsten Wörter notierte er zur Sicherheit gleich auf dem Ausdruck.

neighborhood = Nachbarschaft, Wohngebiet
suburb = Vorort
African American = Amerikaner mit afrikanischen Vorfahren
Caucasian = Amerikaner mit europäischen Vorfahren
Hispanic = Amerikaner mit südamerikanischen Vorfahren
Asian American = Amerikaner mit asiatischen Vorfahren
Extracurricular = außerhalb des normalen Unterrichts
Student Government = Schülervertretung
Principal = Schulleiter

Nico schloss das Fenster wieder und machte sich daran, die erste E-Mail an die McMannons zu verfassen. Gar nicht so einfach, völlig fremden Leuten eine E-Mail zu schreiben. Und dann auch noch auf Englisch ... Vorsichtshalber nahm er wieder das Wörterbuch zu Hilfe. Es dauerte fast eine halbe Stunde, bis Nico mit dem Ergebnis zufrieden war und er auf «absenden» drückte.

To: The McMannon Family
From: Nicolas Wagner
Subject: Hello from Germany!

Dear Mr and Mrs McMannon,
My name is Nicolas Wagner. I'm from Germany. I got a letter today that said that you are my host family in America. I'm very happy and excited!
I want to tell you a little bit about myself. My nickname is Nico. I'm 15 years old and I am a pupil. I will be in year 10 after the summer holidays. My mother is a journalist and my father is an engineer. I don't have any brothers or sisters.
I really like football – I play every day and I like watching it on TV, too. Football is the best sport in the world, I believe. It's also my biggest hobby.
Do you have any children? Will I go to school with them? And do you know my time-table?
It would be great if you could answer my e-mail.
Nicolas Wagner

Ob die McMannons seine Mail wohl gleich sehen würden? Und ob sie ihm dann auch gleich antworteten? Hoffentlich waren sie nett. Und hoffentlich hatten sie einen Sohn in seinem Alter! Nico machte den Computer aus, denn jetzt konnte er nur noch abwarten. Er beschloss, das Kofferpacken auf den nächsten Tag zu verschieben und stattdessen noch ein bisschen im Garten zu kicken. Amerika hin oder her, Fußball spielen musste einfach sein. Und schließlich musste er ja üben – für seine neue Mannschaft und seine neuen Freunde in Amerika!

As ususal, Ashley and Kimmy were spending the evening together. Tonight, they were at the McMannons' house.

«So did you like our cheerleading practice?» Ashley asked Kimmy as the two girls plopped down on the couch in the living room.

«You guys are really good. Even better than last year!» Kimmy nodded. «And I think you're really going to like my article. Do you want to read it?»

«You already finished writing it?» Ashley asked, surprised.

Kimmy nodded. «Sure, it's already online – I uploaded it to the Express website an hour ago.»

«Wow, you're so fast! How do you do that? I could never just write an article for the whole world to read, in … a few hours!» Ashley looked at her friend admiringly.

«Well,» Kimmy said, «maybe I'm a better writer than you. But then,» she grinned, «*I* could never be a cheerleader. And *you* are a fantastic cheerleader!» She paused and then continued, «Come on, I'll show you the article.» She pointed to the laptop that was sitting on the coffee table in front of them.

That moment, the door to the living room opened and Zach burst into the room. As always, he looked like he was ready to play sports: He wore black sweatpants, running shoes and a dark blue football shirt that showed off his wide shoulders. Over his curly brown hair he had put a blue cap.

«Hey,» he said more to Kimmy than to his sister.

Ashley rolled her eyes at Kimmy and pretended not to see him. Quickly, before Kimmy could say hello to Zach, she continued talking.

«Let's see the article,» she said and leaned forward to pick up the laptop. But Zach was faster and grabbed the computer before Ashley could reach it.

«Zach!» she protested. «We were going to read Kimmy's cheerleading article online!»

«Hhmm,» Zach said, uninterested, and looked straight at the laptop. «Whatever. I just want to check something quick.»

«Hello, Zach,» Kimmy said in a more friendly voice.

«Hey,» he said, looking up from the laptop for a second.

«What's going on?» Kimmy tried, but Zach wasn't really paying attention.

«I just need to check my e-mail really quickly,» he said. «There might be news from the coach about football practice.»

«AAAAAH!» Ashley said, rolling her eyes again. «Football practice! My favorite topic. Tell us more,» she said sarcastically.

«Oh, come on, Ashley,» Zach answered and looked at his sister. «Football is the best. I mean, without us football players, you cheerleaders would have nothing to cheer for!»

«YOU come on!» Ashley answered angrily. «Cheerleading is so much more than that. It's the best sport in the world!»

«Yeah, great. Whatever.» Zach mumbled, put the laptop back on the table and got up. «I have to go. Practice starts in 20 minutes. See ya later.»

«Whatever,» Ashley said.

«See you later, Zach,» Kimmy said and smiled to herself as she looked from Ashley to Zach. It was kind of entertaining that the two could never manage to get along.

The moment Zach left the room, Ashley grabbed the laptop.

«What's the address for the school newspaper?» she asked. «I really want to see your article.»

«It's www.jeffersonhigh ...» Kimmy started but was interrupted.

«Oh, good! There's my laptop. Hi, girls,» Mr McMannon had walked into the living room.

«Hey, Dad,» Ashley answered.

«Hi, Mr McMannon,» Kimmy said.

«Sorry, girls, but I really need to check my e-mail really quickly,» Mr McMannon said. «It'll only take a second. You can have the laptop back right away.»

Ashley handed the computer to her dad. «Checking e-mail is pretty popular today, it seems,» she said snappily.

«Huh?» her Dad said as a looked at the computer screen.

«Zach was in here a moment ago, and he checked his e-mail, too.» Kimmy explained. But like his son before him, Mr McMannon wasn't really listening.

«Girls!» he shouted excitedly, «you should see this! We have an e-mail from the German boy! His name is … Nico. He's 15, just like you two!»

«Boring,» Ashley said.

«Cool!» Kimmy answered, sounding really excited.

Mr McMannon grabbed the computer and got up. «I'm going to show this to your mom,» he said as he walked out of the room. «And then I'll write … Nico … back right away. See ya later girls!»

«Looks like I'll never get to read your article in this house,» Ashley said grumpily.

Eigentlich hatte sich Nico vorgenommen, erst am nächsten Morgen nach neuen E-Mails zu gucken. Aber bevor er ins Bett ging, wurde die Neugier doch zu groß. Vielleicht hatten seine Gasteltern ja doch schon geschrieben? Wieder setzte er sich an seinen Schreibtisch, fuhr den Computer hoch und wartete, bis das E-Mail-Postfach erschien. Und … tatsächlich – eine neue Mail. Von den McMannons!

To: Nicolas Wagner
From: The McMannon Family
Subject: Re: Hello from Germany!

Dear Nico,
it was wonderful to hear from you. We're very excited that you will be staying with us.

It was great to learn more about you. You will be happy to hear that our daughter, Ashley, is 15 like you. She is a cheerleader and a very nice girl.

Hier hörte Nico kurz auf zu lesen. Eine Tochter, na ja. Ein Sohn wäre ihm lieber gewesen, aber da konnte man nichts machen. Wenn sie ein Cheerleader war, dachte Nico dann, war sie sicher wenigstens richtig hübsch … oder, na ja, vielleicht auch ziemlich eingebildet. Nico kräuselte die Stirn. Erst mal weiter im Text.

We also have a son: His name is Zachary, but everyone calls him Zach. He's 16 and, like you, he loves playing football! His high school team, the Jefferson Patriots, are fantastic! Maybe you can train with them. Either way, we are sure you two will have a lot to talk about.

Volltreffer, dachte Nico begeistert. Dann las er weiter.

You will be going to Jefferson High School with our kids and we think that it will be no problem at all. Your English is very good, Nico! We noticed, however, that you used some words that we do not use in America. (Maybe it's because you learn British English in school in Germany?) In the USA, we say that you will be in «grade» 10, not «year» 10, and we use the word «student», not «pupil». We also say «summer vacation» and not «summer holiday». We hope this will help you when you come to America.

Oh, there's one more thing: When you asked for your time-table, did you mean your schedule? Your classes at school? We don't know your schedule yet, but you will find it out on your first day at school.

Let us know when you are coming in so we can pick you up from the airport!

Love,

June-Marie and Bruce McMannon

Oh nein, dachte Nico, während er die letzten Zeilen der E-Mail las. Da hatte er ewig über seiner Mail gebrütet, und trotzdem hatte er lauter Wörter verwendet, die in den USA niemand benutzte … Ein bisschen peinlich war das schon! Hoffentlich verstehe ich das Englisch in North Carolina überhaupt, dachte Nico und gruselte sich etwas. Trotz der großen Freude darüber, dass sein Gastbruder nicht nur fast genauso alt wie er, sondern dazu auch noch Fußballer war, fühlte er sich gerade alles andere als gut. Ein halbes Jahr nur noch Englisch sprechen!, dachte er zum ersten Mal, die reden da sicher alle total schnell und mit komischem Akzent und verwenden lauter Wörter, die ich noch nie gehört habe … Nico malte sich lauter peinliche Situationen aus, in denen er rein gar nicht verstand, was sein Gegenüber sagte. Dann atmete er tief durch. Wird schon nicht so schlimm werden, dachte er, hoffentlich!

Kapitel drei –
Get ready!

The next day, Kimmy and Ashley were sitting on the front porch of the McMannon's house. It was very hot, so the two girls were drinking big glasses of iced tea. They were talking about the German exchange student.

«It's going to be so interesting to meet someone from a different country,» Kimmy said excitedly. «Do you think he speaks English well?»

«My parents said his English sounded great in his e-mail,» Ashley answered, sounding bored. «But he did use some funny words, you know, words we don't use here in the US. Like, he said he was a ‹pupil›. Can you believe that? He sounds like the Queen of England!» she laughed.

«Oh come on, don't be mean,» Kimmy said, «remember when you tried to speak German yesterday?»

«Njet!» Ashley answered, now laughing at her own mistake.

Kimmy had to smile, too. «Anyway, I'm sure he's a really nice guy.»

«I don't care,» Ashley declared. «I don't want another brother. And remember what he wrote in that e-mail? He loves football! He thinks football is the best thing in the world! You know what that means: He's going to be exactly like my brother!»

«Oh, come on, Zach isn't that bad,» Kimmy said. «Why do you two always have to fight anyway?»

Ashley looked at Kimmy as if she had gone crazy. «Zach isn't that bad?? He's so stupid. He gets on my nerves so much. Besides, *I* don't want to fight with him, *he* always fights with me!»

«OK,» Kimmy said, not sounding convinced. «Anyway, we decided that things between you and Zach are going to be a lot better when your new German brother arrives, remember? What's his name again?»

«Nicolas, or Nico, or something like that,» Ashley grumbled. «I really hope you're right and the German boy won't go on my nerves! I'm not interested in some guy from Germany!»

«I think it's going to be great,» Kimmy said. «I'd love to have a host brother from Germany.»

«You can have him,» Ashley said snappily. Kimmy grinned.

Ashley, bored with the topic, thought of something new to talk about. «Hey, I have an idea!» she said next. «My parents are at work, Zach is at football practice – yes, again!» She rolled her eyes, «We have the laptop to ourselves, I can read your cheerleading article, finally.»

«Good idea,» Kimmy replied. The girls went inside, found the computer and sat down on Ashley's bed. On the Jefferson High School homepage they clicked the link for the «Express», the High School newspaper. Ashley spotted Kimmy's article at once. It was the first article on the website. Ashley clicked on the headline and read the article.

«Wow,» she exclaimed after she had finished. «That's a fantastic article. And I love the photos you took. I look really cute in this one!»

«Thanks, Ash,» Kimmy replied with a smile. «You know, I love our school, and I love writing about all our activities, cheerleading, football, everything … I love talking to all the students and the teachers and to hear what everybody thinks, and to …»

«Hey!» Ashley cut Kimmy short. «What's this? I've never seen that before!»

Kimmy looked at the screen, surprised. There was a red box on top of her article. It had not been there the day before.

The box read, in big black letters:

DO YOU HAVE THE POWER?

«I don't know what that is,» Ashley said. «Let's click on it!»

Ashley clicked on the red box. A new page opened.

DO YOU HAVE THE POWER?
DO YOU LOVE JEFF HIGH?
DO YOU HAVE WHAT IT TAKES
… TO BE CLASS PRESIDENT?

Students of Jefferson High: class president elections are coming up!

If you love talking to people, if you want to work for your fellow students, if you have exciting ideas to make Jefferson High an even better place:

RUN FOR CLASS PRESIDENT!

«Kimmy, that's it!» Ashley shouted excitedly. «You have to do it. You'd be the perfect class president!»

Viele tausend Kilometer entfernt stand Nico ratlos vor einem extragroßen Überseekoffer. Seine Mutter hatte ihn aus dem Keller geholt, damit er schon einmal mit dem Packen beginnen konnte. Das Wichtigste hatte Nico schon eingepackt. Zuallererst die Fußballklamotten: Schuhe, Trainingshosen, Stutzen, die Trikots seiner Lieblingsmannschaften und – na klar! – das seines eigenen Vereins waren in den Koffer gewandert. Danach hatte er noch einige Jeans, T-Shirts und Pullover hineingeworfen. Weiter war er bisher noch nicht gekommen. Außerdem spukte ihm immer noch die E-Mail vom letzten Abend im Kopf herum … Hoffentlich war sein Englisch wirklich gut genug! Wenn er schon beim Schreiben so viele falsche Wörter benutzt hatte, wie sollte das erst werden, wenn er mit Leuten reden sollte?

Nicos Vater lugte durch die halb offene Tür ins Zimmer. «Na, wie kommst du voran?»

«Es geht. Aber die Hauptsache ist, dass ich nichts von meinen Fußball-Sachen vergesse!» Nico grinste.

«Ach ja? Hast du schon herausgefunden, ob du dort auch in einer Mannschaft spielen kannst?», fragte Herr Wagner interessiert, denn auch er war großer Fußball-Fan.

«Es gibt ein Team an meiner Schule!», erzählte Nico. «Die ‹Jefferson Patriots!› Bestimmt kann ich da mittrainieren. Und das Beste ist: Mein Gastbruder, Zach, spielt da auch!»

«Da hat die Austauschorganisation ja genau die richtige Familie für dich ausgesucht», lachte Nicos Vater und klopfte seinem Sohn auf die Schulter.

Kimmy looked at her friend, totally perplexed. «You really think that *I* should be class president?»

«Totally!» Ashley nodded her head excitedly.

Kimmy looked at the computer screen. «Really?»

«Absolutely, you have to run!» she said. «I mean, you just said it yourself: You love our school, you love talking to people, you know everyone. You're the perfect candidate!»

Kimmy was about to reply something when the door to Ashley's room burst open.

«Zach! Can't you knock before you come in?» Ashley looked at her brother angrily.

«I need the laptop,» he said coolly.

«You can't just come into my room like that.» Ashley stayed on topic.

«Yeah, sorry,» Zach said, not sounding sorry at all. «Laptop, please?»

«You're so rude!» Ashley screetched, holding on to the computer. «What do you need it for anyway?»

«I want to see if that German guy wrote another e-mail,» he replied. «Dad gave me the password to his e-mail account so I can check.»

«Since when are *you* interested in other people anyway?» Ashley asked sharply.

As always, Kimmy tried to make the atmosphere between Ashley and Zach more friendly.

«Great idea, Zach,» she said excitedly. «We want to hear more about the German boy, too. Right, Ashley?»

«Uuhmm, no?» Ashley rolled her eyes. Zach tried to grab the laptop, but she held on to it tightly.

«Dad said the German boy wrote that he is into football,» Zach said to Kimmy in a normal voice. «What's his name again?»

Ashley ignored the question.

«Nico,» Kimmy said.

«Right, Nico. Anyway, Dad said Nico is a football player! I really want to learn more about him. Because I'm into football, too, and you know, the team could always use a good player.»

«Oh really, Zach, you like football? I had no idea! Tell us more!» Ashley said sarcastically.

«Let's check for a new e-mail,» Kimmy jumped in quickly.

«Don't take the laptop with you, Zach,» Ashley said coolly. «Do it here.»

«Alright,» Zach said and flung himself down on the bed in between the girls.

Kimmy could tell that Ashley really wasn't interested in finding out if the German boy had written another e-mail. But she gave Zach the laptop anyway, and without another comment. Kimmy smiled to herself. She had managed to get Ashley and Zach to stop fighting, at least for that moment!

Zach logged in to his father's account and checked the inbox: Nothing. Only some boring e-mails from Mr McMannon's colleagues from work.

«No news from Germany,» Zach sounded a little disappointed.

«I guess your new brother is too busy getting ready for his big trip ...» Kimmy smiled.

Kimmy konnte nicht ahnen, wie richtig sie mit ihrer Vermutung lag: Nico war tatsächlich schwer beschäftigt. Sein Koffer war gepackt, sein Zimmer aufgeräumt, und allen Verwandten, die in der Nähe wohnten, hatte er noch einen Besuch abgestattet. Auch von den meisten seiner Klassenkameraden hatte er sich schon verabschiedet. Jetzt, nach dem letzten Spiel mit seiner Fußballmannschaft, sollte es eine große Abschiedsparty geben. Das Team hatte 2:0 gewonnen, es gab also doppelt Grund zu feiern.

Eigentlich hatte Nico vorgeschlagen, original amerikanische Hamburger für seine Party mitzubringen. Doch seine Mutter hatte andere Pläne. «Bratwurst und Kartoffelsalat», hatte sie am Abend vor der Party verkündet. «Damit du nochmal ein richtig traditionelles deutsches Essen bekommst. Und den anderen Fußballern schmeckt das sicher auch.» Von diesen Argumenten hatte Nico sich sofort umstimmen lassen. Hamburger würde er sicher bald jeden Tag essen! Und von Bratwurst und Kartoffelsalat hatten die Amis in North Carolina sicher noch nie etwas gehört.

Als Nico sich auf seiner Abschiedsparty in einem ruhigen

Moment umguckte, wurde ihm wieder ganz schön seltsam zumute. Klar, er freute sich riesig auf seinen Austausch, aber besonders seine Freunde in der Fußballmannschaft würde er ganz schön vermissen. Für ganze sechs Monate konnte er nicht mit ihnen trainieren!

«Jungs, mal kurz Ruhe, bitte!», rief der Trainer in diesem Moment. «Wir haben doch noch etwas für Nico vorbereitet.»

Während die ganze Mannschaft sich um Nico versammelte, hielt der Trainer eine kurze Rede und überreichte Nico dann ein Mannschaftsfoto und ein Trikot ihres Vereins, auf dem alle Spieler für Nico unterschrieben hatten.

«Viel Spaß in Amerika!», «Nico! Nico!», «Zeig's den Amis!», riefen die anderen Spieler ihm zu, während Nico das Trikot über sein T-Shirt zog und sich bei allen bedankte. Dann betrachtete er das Foto. Die ganze Mannschaft war abgebildet, richtig professionell sah das Bild aus. Ein Reporter der Tageszeitung hatte es vor genau einem Jahr aufgenommen. Mit diesem Abschiedsgeschenk in der Hand fühlte er sich gleich noch mulmiger. Auf dem nächsten Teamfoto würde er nicht zu sehen sein …

Als er so gedankenverloren auf das Bild starrte, trat der Trainer wieder neben ihn.

«Wird schon werden, Nico», sagte er. «Das wird sicher eine Superzeit für dich!»

Nico ließ das Foto sinken und nickte.

«Zeig den Amis, wie man richtig Fußball spielt!», sagte der Trainer, grinste und klopfte ihm auf die Schulter.

Chapter Four –
In Amerika

Zwei Wochen später stand Nico auf dem Flughafen von Charlotte, North Carolina. Er war total übermüdet, denn er hatte ungefähr zehn Stunden Flug hinter sich. Seine Maschine war erst vor ein paar Minuten gelandet, und Nico konnte es kaum glauben: Da draußen, hinter den riesigen Fenstern des Flughafengebäudes, das war wirklich Amerika! Bisher konnte er allerdings nur das riesige Rollfeld sehen und einen strahlend blauen Himmel.

Wie ging es jetzt weiter? Irgendwo wurde sicherlich noch einmal sein Pass kontrolliert, und dann musste er ja auch noch sein Gepäck abholen! Kurz entschlossen folgte er den vielen anderen Reisenden, die mit ihm aus dem Flugzeug gestiegen waren. Alle gingen einen langen Gang hinunter, der viele Kurven machte und kein Ende zu nehmen schien. Dann, endlich, sah er ein Schild, das die Passkontrolle ankündigte. Und tatsächlich: Der Gang endete in einer riesigen Halle, in der vor Passkontrollschaltern lange Schlangen anstanden. Über den Schaltern hingen Schilder, die den Reisenden Orientierung geben sollten. Nico verwirrten sie allerdings eher. «American Citizens and Permanent Residents ONLY» stand da zum Beispiel. Irgendwie klang das nicht so, als ob er sich da anstellen sollte. «Non-Permanent Residents and Visitors» stand auf einem anderen Schild. Nico atmete auf, denn «visitors» war endlich mal ein Wort, das er kannte. Mit vielen anderen Reisenden reihte er sich in die Schlange ein.

Nach einer Wartezeit, die ihm wie eine Ewigkeit erschien und in der die Schlange sich nur im Schneckentempo vorwärtsbewegt hatte, war Nico endlich an der Reihe. Er angelte seine Papiere aus dem Rucksack und trat an den Schalter.

«Hello», sagte er zu dem Mann in Uniform, der ihn streng musterte, während er seinen Pass entgegennahm. Doch der reagierte gar nicht.

«Purpose of stay?», sagte er erst, nachdem er Nicos Pass Seite für Seite durchgeblättert hatte.

Oh nein, dachte Nico. Der erste Kontakt mit einem echten Amerikaner, und sofort war das passiert, wovor er sich gefürchtet hatte: Er hatte nicht die leiseste Ahnung, was der Mann gerade gefragt hatte! «Ähhhmm … sorry?», sagte er deshalb ziemlich kleinlaut.

«Purpose of your visit.» Der Mann sah Nico jetzt direkt in die Augen.

Was zum Teufel bedeutet dieses erste Wort?, dachte Nico verzweifelt. «Ähhhhmm … I … don't understand», versuchte er es.

«WHY ARE YOU HERE?» Der Mann sprach jetzt so langsam und laut, dass die Leute von den anderen Schaltern sich zu Nico umdrehten. Wie peinlich!

«Oh, I'm an exchange student», antwortete er schnell.

«Is that so? How old are you?», fragte der Mann, der jetzt nicht mehr ganz so verkniffen guckte.

«Fifteen», antwortete Nico wie aus der Pistole geschossen.

«And what grade are you in?», kam sofort die nächste Frage.

Nico lächelte, denn das Wort, das der Mann da gerade benutzt hatte, hatte er sich nach der Mail der McMannons extra eingeprägt. «I'm starting the tenth grade», sagte er und fühlte sich ein bisschen selbstbewusster.

«Do you plan to stay in the United States after your exchange program has ended?» Der Beamte musterte Nico jetzt schon wieder ziemlich kritisch.

«No», sagte Nico etwas verunsichert. Was war das denn für eine komische Frage?

«Do you plan to work while you're here?», fragte der Beamte sofort weiter.

«No», antwortete Nico diesmal ganz entschieden. Was wollte dieser Mann denn noch alles wissen?

«You are allowed to be in the United States for 6 months», verkündigte er mit grimmiger Miene und stempelte das Visum in Nicos Pass. «You are clear to stay until February 12th, but not a day longer, understand?»

«Yes … ähhmm, of course.» Nico nickte.

«Enjoy your stay», sagte der Mann und lächelte zum ersten Mal, als er Nico seine Papiere reichte.

«Thank you», sagte Nico erleichtert und wandte sich zum Gehen. «Good-bye!»

«Next!», rief der Beamte in die andere Richtung, als ob Nico gar nicht existierte.

Kopfschüttelnd schulterte Nico seinen Rucksack und machte sich auf die Suche nach der Gepäckausgabe.

«Where is he? Bruce, honey, do you see him?» Mrs McMannon said excitedly as she tried to look through the door through which lots of travellers were coming with their bags and suitcases. The whole McMannon family had driven to the airport to welcome their German exchange student. Mr and Mrs McMannon were holding up a big sign that said «Welcome, Nico!». Zach and Ashley had, for once, agreed that they did not want to hold up any signs.

Unlike her brother, Ashley was very bored. «Maybe that boy over there is Nico?» Ashley offered unenthusiastically and pointed to a boy in a red jacket who was pulling a big suitcase.

«That boy is about 12 years old, Ashley,» Zach said and shook his head. «You're so stupid sometimes!»

«Don't fight, kids,» Mr McMannon tried to stop his children from yet another argument.

«*You*'re stupid,» Ashley snapped at Zach.

«Shut up!» Zach answered.

«*You* shut up!» Ashley retorted.

«Zach, Ashley! Really! Stop fighting, just for once.» Mr McMannon looked at his son and daughter angrily. «We're here to welcome your host brother. Let's all be nice!»

Ashley and Zach said nothing.

«Do you know what Nico looks like?» Zach turned to his mother after a minute or two had passed.

«We saw a picture of him when we talked to the exchange agent a little while ago, don't you remember, darling?» Mrs McMannon said. «In the picture, he had short brown hair. He looked tall and very sporty.»

«I thought all Germans had blond hair,» Ashley said, surprised.

«*You* have blond hair, are *you* German?» Zach asked.

Mr McMannon looked at his children warningly.

«Whatever.» Ashley crossed her arms and looked away.

«That's him! That's Nico!» Mr McMannon suddenly shouted. He pointed to a boy who was walking through the door. He was tall, he had brown hair and was wearing jeans, running shoes and a dark blue sweatshirt. The boy was alone, and he was looking around as if he was trying to find someone.

Nico merkte, wie sein Puls schneller schlug, als er mit seinem Koffer durch die elektrische Schiebetür trat. Überall standen Leute, die Reisende abholten. Vor ihm fiel sich gerade eine Familie in die Arme, und direkt daneben bekam jemand einen riesigen Blumenstrauß überreicht. Wo waren die McMannons? Da! Nico entdeckte ein Plakat mit seinem Namen. Vier Leute standen da: Zwei Erwachsene hielten das Plakat. Daneben stand ein Mädchen mit langen blonden Haaren. Sie sah ziemlich gut aus, das sah Nico sofort, und genau so, wie er sich eine echte amerikanische Cheerleaderin vorgestellt hatte. Aber sie guckte irgendwie ganz schön genervt. Das war dann wohl Ashley. Und daneben, das musste Zach sein, dachte Nico, als er den breitschultrigen Jungen in den Sportklamotten musterte. Wie ein Bodybuilder sah der aus, fuhr es Nico durch den Kopf, gar nicht wie ein Fußballer!

Der Mann, der das Plakat hielt, begann plötzlich aufgeregt mit einem Arm zu fuchteln. Er schien seiner Familie etwas zuzurufen, und plötzlich guckten alle in seine Richtung.

«Hello. I'm Nico», sagte er und trat auf die Familie zu.

«Hello, Nico!», strahlte Mrs McMannon und schloss Nico überschwänglich in ihre Arme. «How are you, *darling*? I'm June-Marie, June-Marie McMannon – call me June-Marie! Or you can call me Mom, if you like! It's so *wonderful* to meet you!»

«Ähhhm, thank you», brachte Nico nur heraus. Er sollte diese wildfremde Frau ‹Mom› nennen? Und hatte sie gerade wirklich ‹Darling› zu ihm gesagt?

«Hi, Nico! Guten Tag!» Mr McMannon reichte Nico die Hand. «Sorry, that's all the German I know … Oh no wait, … Willkommen!» He was smiling. «Bruce McMannon!»

«Hello, Mr McMannon», sagte Nico. Dieser Mann machte schon einen normaleren Eindruck. Immerhin schien er nicht so überdreht wie Mrs McMannon.

«Please, call me Bruce!», sagte Mr McMannon freundlich. «These are our kids, your brother and sister for the next half year, right guys?»

«Hey», sagte das Mädchen betont gelangweilt.

«Hey, what's up. I'm Zach», sagte der Junge um einiges freundlicher.

Nico nickte und lächelte.

«Well, let's get you out of this airport!», sagte Mr McMannon. «Let's go home!»

Nico nickte.

«You got all your bags? You need us to carry anything?», fragte Mr McMannon als Nächstes.

«No thanks», sagte Nico.

«Are you sure, darling? You must be *terribly* tired from your flight!», flötete Mrs McMannon.

«Ähhhm, yes, thank you», antwortete Nico. Diese Mrs McMannon war wirklich ein bisschen seltsam.

Kapitel fünf – **This is Mecklenburg**

Auf dem Weg in sein neues Zuhause kam Nico aus dem Staunen kaum heraus. Gespannt blickte er aus dem Fenster und schaute sich die ungewohnte Umgebung an. Die Gebäude und Straßen sahen irgendwie ganz anders aus als in Deutschland. Und die Autos erst! Es wimmelte nur so von Vans und Pick-up-Trucks. Die wenigen Autos in Normalgröße wirkten auf den breiten Straßen irgendwie verloren. Wie weit die Fahrt bis zum Haus der McMannons wohl sein würde? So richtig nach einer Wohngegend sah es hier zumindest nicht aus, mehr nach einer Autobahn, die abwechselnd durch Wiesen und Industriegebiete führte.

«So you like football?», fragte Zach aus heiterem Himmel.

«Äaaahh, yes», antwortete Nico. «It's great!»

Zach nickte nur zustimmend. Besonders gesprächig schien er nicht zu sein.

«And you?», traute Nico sich, noch eine Frage hinterherzuschieben.

«Football is my life, man», sagte er und grinste zum ersten Mal.

«Mmmh», machte Nico und nickte begeistert. Warum fiel ihm jetzt selber nichts ein, was er noch sagen konnte? Schließlich war Fußball doch sein Lieblingsthema!

«Are you hungry, darling?», mischte Mrs McMannon sich in diesem Moment vom Beifahrersitz ein. Nico zögerte einen Moment, aber Mrs McMannon schien tatsächlich ihn zu meinen.

«A little bit», antwortete er. Eigentlich wollte er hinzufügen, dass es im Flugzeug zwei warme Mahlzeiten gegeben hatte, doch er traute sich nicht so recht. Erst mal nur das unbedingt Nötigste auf Englisch sagen, dachte er sich. Hauptsache, ich benutze nicht wieder völlig falsche Wörter!

«*Fantastic!*», sagte Mrs McMannon in ihrem zuckersüßen Tonfall. «We'll eat dinner the minute we get home.»

«OK», lächelte Nico.

«So, what do you think about Charlotte, Nico?», fragte Mr McMannon vom Fahrersitz.

«I … don't know», sagte Nico zögernd, schließlich hatte er ja noch nicht gerade viel von der Stadt gesehen. «It's … big», sagte er darum diplomatisch.

«You *do* know why the city is named Charlotte, don't you, darling?», fragte Mrs McMannon als Nächstes.

«No», sagte Nico. Das interessierte ihn jetzt wirklich. «Why?»

«Oh, you don't know, honey? It was named after a German queen», erklärte sie. «Queen Charlotte. Have you heard of her?»

«No», sagte Nico überrascht. Von einer deutschen Königin mit diesem Namen hatte er noch nie gehört. Und warum um Himmels willen hatte jemand diese Stadt, die so weit weg von Deutschland lag, nach ihr benannt? Nico versuchte, die Frage im Kopf zu formulieren, doch er gab ziemlich schnell auf. Er war eindeutig zu müde und zu aufgeregt für so komplizierte Fragen.

«So, Mecklenburg County is pretty nice, right?», richtete Mr McMannon wieder das Wort an Nico. Diese Frage verwirrte Nico jetzt völlig. Oder hatte er sich bloß verhört? Mr McMannon musterte ihn freundlich im Rückspiegel. Er musste wohl oder übel antworten.

«I don't know, I mean, I'm not from Mecklenburg», versuchte er zu erklären, «I'm from …»

«Oh, honey, we *know* you're not from Mecklenburg!», fiel Mrs McMannon ihm lachend ins Wort. «*This* is Mecklenburg. The area around Charlotte is called Mecklenburg County.»

«Oh», sagte Nico nur, immer noch sehr verwundert. Erst eine Königin, jetzt noch ein deutsches Gebiet – seltsam! Dabei sah es hier überhaupt nicht deutsch aus. Und die Sprache konnte außer ihm sicherlich auch kein Mensch.

«Interesting», hängte er etwas unbeholfen an, dann wusste Nico nicht mehr, was er noch hätte sagen können. Auch seiner Gastfamilie schien nichts mehr einzufallen. Mr und Mrs McMannon sahen nach vorn durch die Windschutzscheibe,

Zach guckte aus dem Seitenfenster. Und Ashley, die zwischen den beiden Jungen saß, hatte ihren MP3-Player angeschaltet und wippte zur Musik mit.

Nach einer ziemlich langen Zeit, in der sich Nico sehr darauf konzentrieren musste, nicht einzuschlafen, fuhr Mr McMannon in eine hell gepflasterte Einfahrt.

«This is it, Nico. This is our house», sagte Mrs McMannon. «Welcome home!»

Nico betrachtete das Haus, das da vor ihm lag. Es war strahlend weiß, sah ziemlich groß aus, schien aber nur aus einer Etage zu bestehen. Alles wirkte wie im Bilderbuch: Der Rasen im kleinen Vorgarten war sauber getrimmt, der Weg zum Haus wurde von Blumen und Sträuchern gesäumt, und in den Bäumen, die sich in den Himmel reckten, zwitscherten tatsächlich Vögel. Bisher war ihm der ganze Trip ziemlich unwirklich vorgekommen, aber jetzt war er *tatsächlich* angekommen. Das hier war *wirklich* Amerika! Das hier war *wirklich* das Haus, in dem er für die nächsten Monate wohnen würde. Sein neues Zuhause.

«Thank you», sagte er und lächelte zurück.

«Mom, Dad, I'm going to Kimmy's house!» Ashley yelled as she opened the kitchen door.

«But Ashley, honey, don't you want to eat with your new host brother? Dinner is almost ready.» Mrs McMannon pointed to the table that she was setting for five people.

«Uuhmm, I'd love to,» Ashley lied, «but I promised Kimmy

I would …» She paused. «Help her with something! It's … for school! I promised I'd go to her house as soon as we got back from the airport, and I'm already late.»

She turned to her dad who was standing at the stove. «Please, Dad, please!»

«Why not,» Mr McMannon smiled. «If the girls are working for school …?» He looked at his wife.

«Alright, I guess,» Mrs McMannon shrugged. «Don't come home too late, honey.»

«Thanks Mom, thanks Dad,» Ashley said and turned to go so quickly that she almost bumped into Nico and Zach who were on their way into the kitchen.

«Hi, Nico,» she said and waved mockingly, «bye, Nico!» Without another word, she ran across the hall and out the front door.

«Don't mind my little sister, Nico,» Zach said. «She's lame.»

«Zach, darling, please,» Mrs McMannon said. «Why would you say such a thing?»

«It's true, though,» Zach said. «She's so boring! All she ever thinks about is cheerleading, and all she ever does is hang out with Kimmy. Lame!»

«Is Kimmy also a cheerleader?» Nico asked.

«Nope.» Zach shook his head.

«Kimmy is not a cheerleader, honey,» Mrs McMannon jumped in. «But she's a reporter for the school newspaper. And she's Ashley's best friend. She's such a nice girl, isn't she, Zach?»

«Hhhhmm,» Zach said, «she's ok I guess. But she's best friend with my stupid sister, so she can't be …»

«Zach!» Mr McMannon didn't let his son finish his sentence. «Stop it! Why can't you just give Ashley a break? Just for one minute?»

Zach only shrugged his shoulders.

«Nico, dear, why don't you have a seat,» Mrs McMannon changed the subject. «Dinner is ready. I made something simple today, hope you don't mind. You do like brats, don't you, darling?»

«Brats?» Nico repeated. «I don't know, what is ‹brats›?»

«Bratwurst,» Zach said.

«Oh!» Nico said, sounding surprised.

«I made brats and potato salad, hope you like that, Nico?» Mrs McMannon asked again.

«Yes, I do,» Nico said with a big smile as he sat down in one of the chairs.

«So, Nico,» Mr McMannon said and sat down, too. «You told us you like football.»

«Yes!» Nico said.

«We're a football family,» Mr McMannon explained. «I used to play football myself, back in my day, you know,» he chuckled, «and now, Zach here is our football star. He's on the school team: The Jefferson Patriots!»

Zach nodded proudly.

«Cool,» Nico said. He thought for a few seconds. «Is the team … good?»

«Hell yeah!» Zach answered.

«Absolutely,» Mr McMannon said. «The best high school football team in Charlotte!»

«Can I come and …» Nico looked for the right words. «Do you think I can play on your team, too?»

«Don't know, are you any good?» Zach smiled.

«Maybe you can take Nico to football practice on Tuesday after school,» Mr McMannon said. «Then he can see for himself if he's good enough to make the team.»

Nico nodded excitedly.

«Deal,» Zach said and took a big bite out of his bratwurst.

Nach dem Essen, das Nico trotz seiner Müdigkeit richtig gut geschmeckt hatte, ließ er sich von Mr McMannon das Telefon geben. Er wählte – und schon nach kurzem Klingeln wurde am andern Ende der Leitung abgehoben.

«Wagner?», sagte eine ziemlich schläfrige Stimme.

«Mama!», rief Nico aufgeregt in den Hörer.

«Nico, Gott sei Dank, wir warten schon die ganze Zeit, dass du dich endlich meldest!» Seine Mutter klang richtig erleichtert. «Ich muss kurz eingenickt sein …» Sie gähnte.

«Ich bin gut angekommen», sprudelte er hervor, erleichtert, endlich wieder Deutsch sprechen zu können. «Der Flug war ziemlich langweilig, aber die McMannons haben mich abgeholt, ich habe ein ziemlich großes Zimmer, und gegessen haben wir auch schon, und rate mal, was es gab?»

Frau Wagner lachte, als Nico ihr das Abendessen beschrieb. «Das kommt mir allerdings bekannt vor», sagte sie.

«Wusstest du, dass die Stadt hier nach einer deutschen Königin benannt wurde?», fragte Nico. «Und dass die Gegend hier Mecklenburg heißt?»

Auch Frau Wagner war überrascht. Allerdings hatte sie eine Vermutung. «Das liegt sicher daran, dass früher viele deutsche Einwanderer sich dort niedergelassen haben – und dann haben sie die Gegend nach ihrer Heimat benannt», sagte sie.

«Kann sein», sagte Nico, der sich plötzlich wieder sehr, sehr müde fühlte. Er gähnte.

«Kein Wunder, dass du erschöpft bist, nach der langen Reise … und es ist ja auch schon ein Uhr morgens hier in Deutschland.»

Nico sah auf seine Armbanduhr, die er schon im Flieger umgestellt hatte. Sie zeigte an, dass es in Charlotte erst sieben Uhr abends war.

«Ich glaube, ich gehe gleich ins Bett.»

«Mach das, mein Junge», sagte seine Mutter.

«Tschüs, Mama», antwortete er, «und grüß Papa von mir.»

Nachdem er aufgelegt hatte, beschloss er, dass es wirklich die beste Idee war, erst mal zu schlafen, obwohl draußen noch die Sonne vom Himmel strahlte. Morgen war Samstag, es war also noch jede Menge Zeit, die McMannons besser kennenzulernen, bevor die Woche – und damit die Schule – am Montag losging. Zach war nirgendwo zu sehen, aber er wünschte Mr und Mrs McMannon, die zusammen vor dem Fernseher saßen, eine gute Nacht und verdrückte sich dann in sein Zimmer. Er zog die Vorhänge zu und war, kaum, dass er unter die Decke gekrochen war, tief eingeschlafen.

Chapter Six –
Mehr von Charlotte

«There he is!», rief Mr McMannon gut gelaunt, als Nico am nächsten Morgen vorsichtig in die Küche lugte. Seine Gasteltern saßen dort und tranken Kaffee. «We were just talking about you – come in!», fügte er hinzu, bevor Nico reagieren konnte.

«Good morning, darling», sagte dann auch Mrs McMannon und deutete auf den Stuhl neben ihrem. «How are you today? Tell me, dear, would you like some coffee? I understand the Europeans love their coffee even more than we do! We also have tea, or milk. Do you want a bagel with cream cheese? Or an English muffin? Or toast? There is also a blueberry muffin left – oh, and cereal, of course!»

«Ähm, thank you», sagte Nico erst mal nur und setzte sich zu Mr und Mrs McMannon. Das war gleich wieder viel zu viel Englisch auf einmal! Er sah sich auf dem Tisch um. Da standen tatsächlich die ganzen Sachen, die Mrs McMannon gerade aufgezählt hatte. Die kleinen runden Toastbrötchen mussten wohl die English Muffins sein.

«I would like … some toast please, and some milk», sagte er nach einigem Zögern.

«Coming right up», sagte Mr McMannon und angelte den riesigsten Milchcontainer aus dem Kühlschrank, den Nico je gesehen hatte. Das Ding sah aus wie ein Benzinkanister! Nico bedankte sich, schenkte sich ein Glas ein und steckte zwei Scheiben Toast in den Toaster. Jetzt musste er sich wohl oder übel etwas einfallen lassen, über das er mit seinen Gasteltern reden konnte.

«Are Zach and Ashley still asleep?», fragte er, nachdem er ein paar Schlucke der eiskalten Milch getrunken hatte.

«Oh, I'm so sorry honey, but you just missed them», flötete Mrs McMannon.

«Ashley is at Kimmy's house again», erklärte Mr McMannon. «The two are always together – they are practically inseparable, aren't they, June?»

«They sure are», lachte Mrs McMannon.

«And where is Zach?», fragte Nico.

«At the weight room, of course», sagte Mr McMannon, als ob es die klarste Sache der Welt wäre. Nico wusste allerdings gar nicht, was damit gemeint sein könnte.

«The … wait room?», fragte er.

«Weight room! You know! The place where you go to work out, lift weights and so on!», erklärte Mr McMannon.

«Oh, OK», nickte Nico. Gewichte heben am Samstagmorgen, so sah Zach auch aus.

Der Toast poppte aus dem Toaster, und während Nico ihn mit Butter und Marmelade bestrich, ergriff Mrs McMannon wieder das Wort.

»We thought that Bruce could take you for a ride around the city this morning. Or you could come to the supermarket with me and do some grocery shopping! What do you think, honey?»

Darüber brauchte Nico nicht lange nachdenken.

«I think I'd like to see the city», sagte er.

«Alright», sagte Mr McMannon und schlug ihm auf die Schulter. «Why don't you finish your breakfast, and then we get going?»

Nico nickte und biss in seinen Toast.

«If you look to your right», sagte Mr McMannon, als sie eine Viertelstunde später – diesmal mit Nico auf dem Beifahrersitz – über die mehrspurige Straße rollten, «you can see downtown Charlotte.»

Nico bewunderte die vielen Hochhäuser, die sich da aneinanderreihten. Fast erinnerte ihn der Anblick an die Skyline von New York, die er schon oft auf Bildern gesehen hatte.

«Charlotte is a banking city», erklärte Mr McMannon, «and most of those really tall buildings are owned by the banks.»

Die breite Straße wurde zu einer Überführung, die den Verkehr nicht etwa, wie Nico zuerst dachte, über einen Fluss führte, sondern über andere Straßen, die auch auf Brücken ziemlich kurvig über- und untereinander geleitet wurden. Fast wie eine Achterbahn sah das aus. Nico war beeindruckt.

«Over there is the Charlotte Bobcats arena. Have you heard of the Bobcats?», fragte Mr McMannon und zeigte auf ein imposantes Stadion. Nico schüttelte den Kopf.

«They are a pro basketball team», erklärte Mr McMannon, «a really good one. Do you guys play basketball in Germany?»

«Some people do», erklärte Nico. «But football is more popular.»

«I don't know much about Germany, but that does sound good», lachte Mr McMannon.

Nico hatte noch eine Frage. «You said they are a pro basketball team. What does ‹pro› mean?», wollte er wissen.

«‹Pro› means professional», erklärte Mr McMannon bereitwillig. «If you play sports in high school and college, you are not a professional. But if you make it onto the professional teams, if it's your job to play sports, then you're a pro.»

«Oh, OK», sagte Nico. Das leuchtete ihm ein. Er überlegte einen Moment. «After school, I want to be a football pro», sagte er dann und lachte etwas verlegen.

«That's my boy», grinste Mr McMannon zurück.

Dann sagten sie erst mal eine Weile nichts. Nico guckte aus dem Fenster und sah die Skyline von Charlotte immer kleiner werden. Richtig ländlich sah es nach einer Weile aus, Wälder und Wiesen, Felder und ab und zu ein paar Häuser, die sicherlich Bauernhöfe waren, waren da jetzt, wenn er um sich blickte.

«Mecklenburg county has it all», erklärte Mr McMannon. «The big city and some real nice countryside. We also have some great golf courses. Do people in Germany play golf, Nico?»

«Some people do», sagte Nico und grinste wieder, «but football is a lot more popular.»

«Ha!», lachte Mr McMannon, «I'm liking Germany more and more.»

Nico lachte mit. Sein Gastvater war wirklich nett.

«You know what else I like?», fragte der als Nächstes. «Original North Carolina sweet tea.»

Nico guckte erwartungsvoll.

«Do people in Germany drink iced tea?», fragte Mr McMannon.

«Sometimes», sagte Nico. «I really like it!»

«I'm from the North of the US, from Boston», erzählte Mr McMannon. «Up there, we drink iced tea without sugar. Actually, people drink it unsweet in most of the US. Sweet tea is a Southern specialty, you could say. Down here, people add a lot of sugar to their iced tea, and I mean a *lot* of sugar», lachte er. «What do you say? Do you want to try some?»

Nico war froh, im Süden gelandet zu sein. Wer, bitte schön, wollte denn ungesüßten kalten Tee trinken? Nico zumindest nicht. «Yes», sagte er deshalb.

«There's a diner not too far from here, you know, a little restaurant. We can stop for some sweet tea and a snack. I could go for some fried chicken myself. What about you? How about some tea and some real American food?»

Nico hatte zwar gerade erst gefrühstückt, aber er war trotzdem begeistert. «Great!», nickte er.

«Well alright», lachte Mr McMannon und setzte den Blinker. «Some lunch for you and me, and then more sightseeing in Charlotte.»

«Alright!», sagte auch Nico und lachte zurück.

Kapitel sieben –

The first day of school

Before school on Monday morning, Ashley and Kimmy met outside the school building.

«I can't believe the summer is over,» Ashley said, «we're going to have to get up early again – every morning! And I don't even want to think about all the homework.»

«At least we'll be able to see all our friends,» Kimmy said. «And don't forget about cheerleading.»

«Oh, like I'd *ever* forget about cheerleading!» Ashley laughed. «And you, you'll be able to work for the Express.»

«Yeah,» Kimmy nodded, «I already have some great ideas for new articles.»

«And there's something else we can do this year,» Ashley smiled.

«Oh, not again …» Kimmy sighed.

«I'm telling you, Kimmy, you just have to do it. You have to run for class president!» Ashley said.

«You've been saying this a million times,» Kimmy laughed, «and it sounds great! But I just don't know if I'm the right person for the job. Plus, I'm already so busy – I never have any time at all!»

«I think you'd be absolutely perfect,» Ashley said. «And I told you, I can help you! I can be on your team!»

«Yes, but …» Kimmy began.

«I'm a cheerleader, Kimmy, and I can get all the other cheerleaders to help. We're the most popular girls in the entire school! We can totally help you win the class presidency,» Ashley continued.

«That sounds fantastic, Ash,» Kimmy said, «I just don't know if I …»

«I'm telling you, you'll be perfect for the job,» Ashley said again. «I can see it clearly: my best friend, the class president!»

«Hey, look who's over there,» Kimmy suddenly pointed to her right. She had spotted Zach walking up to the school. Next to him, there was a boy Kimmy had never seen before. He had brown hair and he was wearing a blue T-Shirt and jeans. That had to be the German exchange student. He looked a little shy, Kimmy thought. But cute … very cute!

«Oh, how exciting, is that Nico?» Kimmy asked.

«Yup,» Ashley said. «Anyway, about the class presidency …»

«Let's talk to him,» Kimmy said, «I want to meet him!»

«Naaaah … You can meet him later,» Ashley said.

«Come on,» Kimmy said. «Introduce me. I've never talked to someone from Germany before, I want to meet Nico *now*!»

Als Nico neben Zach zum ersten Mal auf das große Schulgebäude zuging, sah man dort schon überall Gruppen von Schülern. Viele, die sich wahrscheinlich die ganzen Ferien lang nicht gesehen hatten, fielen sich in die Arme, andere waren in Gespräche vertieft oder gingen lachend mit ihren Freunden vor dem Eingangstor auf und ab. Nico fiel auch noch auf, dass tatsächlich ungefähr die Hälfte der Schüler Afroamerikaner waren. Er sah auch viele weiße Gesichter und hin und wieder jemanden, dessen Familie sicher aus Asien in die USA gekommen war. Und ich bin jetzt der einzige Ausländer an dieser Schule, dachte Nico, als er sich an den Interneteintrag erinnerte. Ein seltsames Gefühl!

Als Zach und er fast vor der Schule angekommen waren, fiel ihm ein riesiges Transparent ins Auge, das über dem Haupteingang gespannt war. ‹Welcome back, Patriots!› stand da. Patriots? Das war doch der Name der Fußballmannschaft!

«Why is there a sign for the football team?», fragte er Zach.

«It's not only for the football team, man!», antwortete der, «it's for everyone.»

Nico war nach dieser Antwort genauso schlau wie vorher, doch irgendwie wollte er nicht noch einmal genauer nachfragen. Bevor er weiter darüber nachdenken konnte, was es mit dem Transparent wohl auf sich hatte, wurde er von etwas anderem abgelenkt.

«Nico!» Zu seiner Überraschung war es Ashley, die ihn das ganze Wochenende kaum beachtet hatte, die da auf ihn zugeschlendert kam. Im Schlepptau hatte sie ein Mädchen. Das war bestimmt Kimmy, Ashleys beste Freundin. Als Erstes fielen Nico ihre unzähligen eng geflochtenen Zöpfe auf, die ihr lang über die dunkelbraunen Arme fielen. Genau wie Ashley trug sie Jeansshorts und ein T-Shirt mit dem Jefferson-High-School-Logo. Allerdings war das Shirt von Kimmy leuchtend grün. Das gefiel Nico deutlich besser als Ashleys Top in babyrosa.

«Hey», sagte Ashley betont gelangweilt, als sie vor ihm stand. Dass Zach auch da war, übersah sie einfach. «I want you to meet my best friend: Kimmy, this is Nico, Nico, this is Kimmy!»

«Hey Nico!» Kimmy strahlte ihn an. «It's so nice to meet you! How are you?»

«Hello», sagte Nico etwas schüchtern. Diese Kimmy war aus der Nähe noch hübscher, als er gedacht hatte. Und hundertmal netter als Ashley wirkte sie auch noch! «Ähhm, I'm fine, thank you», hängte er dann noch etwas unbeholfen an.

«So, how do you like Charlotte? You must be so excited to be here!», sprudelte Kimmy sofort los.

«It's … nice», antwortete Nico.

«And do you like the McMannons? Aren't they great?», fragte Kimmy als Nächstes.

Nico warf einen kurzen Blick auf seine Gastgeschwister, die sich immer noch vollkommen ignorierten. Beide schienen keine Lust zu haben, sich am Gespräch zu beteiligen.

«Yes», sagte er schnell. Vielleicht sollte er Kimmy auch mal eine Frage stellen? Zum Glück fiel ihm – ausnahmsweise – gleich etwas ein.

«Are you in the 10th grade?», fragte er.

«Yeah», sie nickte, «I'm a sophomore, like Ashley and you.»

«A sopho …?», fragte Nico verdutzt.

«So-pho-more», betonte Kimmy das Wort Silbe für Silbe. «It's our word for students in the tenth grade.»

Nico nickte. Noch so ein Wort, das er im Englischunterricht noch nie gehört hatte. Zumindest konnte er sich nicht daran erinnern. Eins war allerdings klar, wenn er, Nico, ein «Sophomore» war, sollte er sich das Wort besser merken!

Plötzlich schien Ashley etwas einzufallen.

«Oh! We haven't told you guys yet!» Zu Nicos Überraschung wandte sie sich jetzt sogar an Zach. Es musste wohl etwas wirklich Wichtiges sein. «Kimmy is going to run for sophomore class president! Isn't that totally cool?»

Kimmy guckte, als wollte sie etwas einwenden, doch Zach antwortete zuerst.

«Cool!», sagte er und klang für seine Verhältnisse sogar wirklich einigermaßen beeindruckt. Dann sah er auf seine Uhr. «Gotta go. See ya later.» Mit diesen Worten verschwand er in der Menge der Schüler.

«What's a class president?», fragte Nico die beiden Mädchen. Aus der langwierigen Erklärung, bei der Kimmy und Ashley sich immer wieder begeistert ins Wort fielen, schloss er, dass ein ‹class president› nichts anderes als ein Jahrgangssprecher war. Aufregend klang das in seinen Ohren nicht gerade – eher im Gegenteil!

«Okay», sagte er deswegen nur. Er wollte sich mit Kimmy lieber wieder über etwas anderes unterhalten. Was könnte er sie bloß noch fragen? Er guckte sich um, und dabei fiel ihm wieder das Transparent über dem Eingang ins Auge.

«Is that sign for the football team?», stellte er seine Frage von vorhin einfach noch einmal. Im Gegensatz zu Zach gab Kimmy gleich bereitwillig Auskunft.

«It's for all of the students here. The football team is called the Jefferson Patriots, but all other teams are called that, too:

the basketball team, the wrestling team, the swimming team and so on», fügte sie deswegen hinzu. «In fact, every student who goes to Jefferson High is a Jefferson Patriot!»

«Okay», sagte Nico etwas zögerlich. Kimmy strahlte ihn schon wieder an.

«That means», sagte er ermutigt, «that I'm a Jefferson Patriot now, too!»

«That's right», sagte sie. Sie lächelten sich ein paar Sekunden an, ohne etwas zu sagen.

Dann ergriff Ashley wieder das Wort. «Come on, Kimmy, let's go inside, class begins in 5 minutes.» Sie hakte Kimmy unter und zog sie in Richtung Eingang. Nico blieb nichts anderes übrig, als den Mädchen ins Schulgebäude zu folgen. Noch fünf Minuten, dann begann sein erster Tag als Schüler einer amerikanischen High School oder, wie er gerade gelernt hatte, sein erster Tag als waschechter Jefferson Patriot.

At noon, after a morning of classes, Kimmy was in a great mood. All through class, Ashley had told everybody – *really every last person* – about her idea that Kimmy should run for class president.

«Kimmy, you'd be perfect as class president,» many people had answered.

«I'll vote for you!» others had said.

«Kimmy for president!» somebody had shouted.

Even Ms Hebig, the Geography teacher, joined the conversation. «Ashley's idea sounds great, Kimmy,» she said.

«You're a reporter for the Express, you're a good student, you have a lot of friends. You'd have great chances at winning the election!»

«I know!» Ashley beamed at her best friend. «What have I been telling you?»

As Kimmy walked to the cafeteria with Ashley and Nico to eat some lunch, she felt more and more excited. It was true, she was much too busy already; but for the first time, she felt that she could still do it. She could run for sophomore class president! She could *be* class president! She could make the school a better place – for everyone! She could organize parties for all the sophomores, or she could start a project in which sophomores helped younger students with their homework, or a project in which sophomores collected money to help poor people, or …

«Can I help you?» An unfriendly voice interrupted her thoughts.

Kimmy looked up. She had been so lost in daydreaming that she hadn't noticed that she was next in the lunch line at the cafeteria.

«What d'you want?» the woman asked.

«Uuhmm, I'll have the brats, and some potato salad,» Kimmy said quickly. The woman put the food on a tray and handed it to her.

Ashley, who was standing right behind her, asked for some chips and a chocolate bar, which the woman handed to her without another word.

Then it was Nico's turn.

«Bratwurst, please.» Kimmy heard him say. The word sounded very German.

«Huh?» the unfriendly woman said.

«Bratwurst,» he said again, a little louder, but sounding very German again, «please.» Kimmy saw that his cheeks had turned a little pink.

«*What* d'you want?» the woman asked almost angrily.

Nico seemed lost for words. He looked around helplessly.

«The same food she has.» Nico finally said and pointed to Kimmy's tray.

«Oh, *bratwurst,*» the woman said the word with a strong American accent, «why didn't you say that?»

Kimmy caught Nico's eye, and they both couldn't help but laugh out loud.

Chapter Eight – **Viele Infos**

Während er mit den beiden Mädchen in der Cafeteria saß, sah Nico sich neugierig um: So viele unbekannte Gesichter, so viele Stimmen, und von überall her klang Gelächter. Auch Ashley redete unaufhörlich, allerdings ganz deutlich nicht mit ihm, sondern nur mit Kimmy. Das fand Nico gar nicht so schlimm, denn bei Ashleys Tempo konnte er ohnehin nur die Hälfte verstehen. Es schien aber wieder um die Jahrgangssprecherwahlen zu gehen. Plötzlich unterbrach Ashley ihren Redefluss.

«Oh, there are the other girls!», sagte sie und sprang auf. «I'll be right back.»

«Those are the other cheerleaders», erklärte Kimmy Nico. «They usually all eat lunch together. All the cheerleaders, Ashley, and, well, me.»

Nico nickte.

«So how's your *bratwurst*?», fragte sie dann und versuchte grinsend, das Wort richtig deutsch auszusprechen.

«My *bratwurst*», Nico gab sich Mühe, besonders amerikanisch zu klingen, «is good.» Beide lachten.

«It must be funny for you when we use German words in English», sagte Kimmy als Nächstes.

Nico kaute und nickte.

«Are there many people from Germany in Charlotte?», fragte er dann, denn diese Kimmy schien sich ziemlich gut auszukennen.

«Sure», antwortete Kimmy, «there are lots of Germans. But their families moved here generations ago. Their names are German, but most of them have always been here in the US.»

Nico nickte wieder.

«There are people from all over the world in the US», erklärte Kimmy als Nächstes.

«Mr McMannon's family came from Ireland, for example, and my family is originally from Kenia, in Africa. But», sie grinste, «we're all Americans. Isn't it great?»

«That is great», stimmte Nico ihr zu. Doch er hatte auch eine Frage. Er wusste nicht genau, ob er sie stellen konnte. Aber warum eigentlich nicht?, dachte er dann.

«Are there any problems in Charlotte …», versuchte er es auf Englisch, doch er kriegte den Satz nicht richtig formuliert. «between … people …»

Zum Glück schien Kimmy zu ahnen, was er fragen wollte.

«Do you mean, is there racism? Are there problems between white people and black people in Charlotte?», fragte sie zurück.

Nico nickte.

«You know that there used to be slavery in some parts of the USA, don't you?», fragte Kimmy. «My great-great-great grandparents were brought from Africa as slaves», fuhr sie fort. «They were never free. They were owned by white families, and they were treated like things, not people.»

Unglaublich, dachte Nico gebannt. Theoretisch hatte er das natürlich gewusst, aber so richtig hatte er noch nie über das Thema nachgedacht.

«You know», sprach sie weiter, «slavery was supposed to have ended in 1863, but then there was the Civil War, and North Carolina actually fought for the South, so that they could keep having slaves! After the South lost the war, there was a long period of laws against Blacks that didn't end until the 1960s.»

Bis in die sechziger Jahre, dachte Nico, das schien ihm wirklich noch nicht lange her zu sein.

«Even now, there are still a few white people around here who hate», fuhr Kimmy fort. «They hate the North, they hate non-whites, they just … they just pretty much hate everything that's not just like they are.»

Nico sah Kimmy ziemlich entsetzt an.

«We call them rednecks», sprach Kimmy weiter, «or just idiots.» Sie lachte. «You probably won't see many of them around here, in Charlotte. Maybe way, way out in the countryside where they never talk to anyone, but not in the city. Just look around here at Jefferson High, for example, everybody is friends with everyone, nobody cares if you're black or white or from Asia or South America ...»

«... or international!», beendete Nico lachend ihren Satz.

«Exactly», lachte auch Kimmy. «I think you're going to fit right in, Nico!»

«I hope so», antwortete Nico.

«How are you getting along with everybody anyway?», wollte Kimmy wissen. «You're meeting so many new people!»

«Mr and Mrs McMannon are very nice», antwortete Nico, «and everyone at the school seems nice, too.» Allerdings war bisher noch niemand so nett gewesen wie dieses Mädchen hier, schoss es Nico durch den Kopf.

«And how about Zach?», fragte Kimmy als Nächstes.

«I don't know», gab Nico zu. Irgendwie hatte er das Gefühl, dass er Kimmy die Wahrheit sagen konnte. «He hasn't said much. Is he always so ... quiet?»

«Yeah», Kimmy lachte. «He's usually pretty quiet. He's not a talker – but he's a great football player, you know.»

«Me too», lächelte Nico stolz.

«That's right! Well, then I'm sure you and Zach will be friends. Just give him some time», sagte sie aufmunternd.

Nico nickte. Es war gut, mit jemandem zu sprechen, der

seine Gastfamilie besser kannte. Nico bemerkte, dass Kimmy noch irgendetwas loswerden wollte. Sie guckte sich um, ob Ashley noch bei den anderen Cheerleadern stand, dann drehte sie sich wieder zu Nico.

«Have you noticed that … Ashley and Zach … well, have you noticed that they don't get along too well?», fragte sie vorsichtig. «To be honest, they fight all the time.»

Nico nickte. Dass die Stimmung zwischen den Geschwistern richtig schlecht war, hatte er schnell gemerkt.

«The reason I'm telling you this», fuhr Kimmy fort, «is that … well …» Sie zögerte. «Ashley is my best friend. I've known her since kindergarten. But … she can be a little snappy sometimes. Sometimes people think she's arrogant, or unfriendly. And, well, it's true that she is pretty unfriendly towards Zach!» Kimmy lachte.

Nico nickte wieder. «Ashley hasn't really talked to me at all», gab er zu.

Jetzt nickte Kimmy. «I guess what I'm trying to say is, Ashley is a nice girl. She may seem a little cold and snappy, but she's a great person. My point is, I think she might need some time to get used to having a second brother!»

«OK», sagte Nico. Das leuchtete ihm irgendwie ein. Richtig glücklich war er nicht über seine Gastgeschwister, aber vielleicht hatte Kimmy ja recht und es würde bald alles entspannter laufen.

«They are so different from each other», sagte Kimmy. «Usually, football players and cheerleaders are a great match – but not Zach and Ashley. They are like cat and mouse!»

Kimmy und Nico hatten gar nicht bemerkt, dass Ashley wieder an den Tisch getreten war.

«Me and Zach? Cat and mouse? Please!», sagte sie gut gelaunt und selbstbewusst. «More like the beauty and the beast!»

To: Familie Wagner
From: Nico Wagner
Subject: Hallo aus Charlotte

Hallo, Mama und Papa,
jetzt ist es abends, und ich bin schon wieder total müde, aber ich wollte mich nochmal kurz melden, weil wir ja gar nicht mehr telefoniert haben, seit ich angekommen bin. Ich hatte heute meinen ersten Schultag! Es war ganz gut: Ich habe das meiste verstanden, und die anderen in der Schule waren auch ganz nett. Die Schule ist riesengroß, und man ist bei jedem Fach mit anderen Schülern zusammen. Ich habe mich fast nach jeder Stunde erst mal verlaufen!
Meine Gastgeschwister reden immer noch nicht so viel mit mir, aber ich habe die beste Freundin von Ashley kennengelernt, und die hat mir in der Schule viel erklärt. Und weißt du was, Mama, heute gab es in der Cafeteria Bratwurst und Kartoffelsalat! Dieses Essen verfolgt mich.
Morgen gehe ich zum ersten Mal zum Fußballtraining!
Bis bald,
Euer Nico

Kapitel neun –

Oh, football!

Der zweite Tag in der neuen Schule war für Nico viel anstrengender als der erste. Am Montag hatten sich alle noch über die langen Sommerferien ausgetauscht, und im Unterricht war noch nicht viel passiert. Viele Schüler und die meisten Lehrer hatten es interessanter gefunden, Nico, dem Neuen aus dem fremden Land, Fragen zu stellen.

«What is Germany like?»

«Do you like Charlotte?»

«Have you been to the US before?»

«Is our school a lot like your school in Germany?»

Nico hatte viel zu tun gehabt, alle Fragen zu beantworten. Erst war es ihm etwas unangenehm gewesen, so im Mittelpunkt zu stehen. Doch mit der Zeit, nachdem er immer mehr auf Englisch gesagt hatte und die anderen ihn tatsächlich zu verstehen schienen, hatte er sich besser gefühlt. Es schien, als würden sich alle wirklich für ihn, den «German boy», interessieren!

Ein Mädchen aus seinem Erdkundekurs hatte sogar kichernd gefragt: «Do you have a girlfriend in Germany, Nico?»

Er war rot angelaufen und hatte ein kurzes «No» gemurmelt, was viele Schüler zum Lachen gebracht hatte. Nur Ashley schien das Ganze irgendwie zu langweilen. Nico bemerkte, dass sie, sobald es irgendwie eine Möglichkeit gab, das Thema wechselte und wieder von dieser Jahrgangssprecherwahl anfing. Auch die anderen Schüler schienen das ein spannendes

Thema zu finden, und so wurde es am ersten Schultag nie langweilig.

Der Dienstag aber sah für Nico anders aus. Austauschüler hin oder her, nun begann der Ernst des Unterrichts. Nico musste sich ganz schön konzentrieren, um überall wenigstens einigermaßen mitzukommen. Schon in der dritten Stunde war er so erledigt, dass er auf der Stelle hätte einschlafen können. Am liebsten wäre er nach Hause gegangen und hätte sich wieder in sein Bett verkrochen. Doch zum Glück gab es etwas, das ihm genug Energie gab, den Vormittag durchzustehen: Heute Nachmittag war es endlich so weit: Zach würde ihn mitnehmen zum ersten offiziellen Fußball-Training im neuen Schuljahr. Schon beim Gedanken daran kribbelte es in Nicos Beinen. Endlich konnte er wieder auf den Platz und zeigen, was er draufhatte.

Nach der letzten Stunde, die Nico wie eine Ewigkeit vorgekommen war, wartete Zach vor der Klassentür.

«Everything alright, man?», rief er und ging grinsend auf Nico zu, der gerade seine Sporttasche schulterte.

«You got all your stuff in that small bag?», fragte Zach und deutete auf die Tasche. Er selber hatte eine Tasche dabei, die fast so groß war wie Nicos Überseekoffer.

«Yes», sagte Nico zögerlich. Hatte er etwa irgendetwas vergessen?

«OK … let's go», erwiderte Zach, warf die schwere Tasche über seine breiten Schultern und ging voraus. «I can't wait to play football again. I mean, for real! Training is one thing – but the games – man, I love the games!»

Nico konnte Zachs Begeisterung gut verstehen.

«Our team was great last year! I had a good year, too», sagte Zach und klang richtig stolz, «so good that some of the other players started calling me Sweetness, like Walter Payton!»

«Walter who?» Nico hatte den Namen noch nie gehört. Oder hatte er Zach nur falsch verstanden? Doch Zach hatte Nicos Frage wohl nicht ernst genommen. Er lachte nur und ging mit großen Schritten den Gang hinunter in Richtung der riesigen Sportanlagen.

At the same moment, Kimmy and Ashley were also walking onto the school's athletic fields. Ashley was going to cheerleading practice. Kimmy, who had a camera and a note pad in her hand, was working for the Express. In the next edition of the newspaper, there was going to be an article on each of the Jefferson Patriot sports teams. Kimmy had asked to write about the cheerleaders again and was now trying to interview her best friend about the cheerleading squad.

Usually, Ashley would have loved nothing better than talking about her sport. Today, however, she had other things on her mind.

«Remember when I got a D in my Spanish test? And I was too scared to ask Mr. Lewis what had gone wrong?» she asked.

«Yes, of course. We went up to him together after class and asked what you could do to get a better grade in the next test,» Kimmy replied, not knowing why Ashley was bringing up this old story.

«I was so glad you helped me,» Ashley explained. «You are so good at talking to teachers! I would never have done that on my own.»

«Why not?» Kimmy asked, surprised. «It was so easy, and Mr Lewis was really nice.»

«Those things are easy for you! It was really embarrassing for me to talk to Mr Lewis about that. In fact, I think it's a hard thing to do for most students.» Ashley smiled. «Which is exactly why you should run for class president!»

Kimmy smiled.

«Oh, and Kimmy,» Ashley continued, «you know how you always try to make me be nicer to Zach? And how you are always friendly to Zach so we don't fight?»

Kimmy nodded. She hadn't thought before that Ashley had even noticed.

«You're so good at that, too! You know how to calm people down and to make them more … relaxed. That's a great thing for a class president!» Ashley said enthusiastically.

Kimmy's smile widened.

«You know, Ash,» she said, «I've been thinking. And I think … you're right. I'm going to run for class president.»

«For real?» Ashley said, stopping in her tracks.

«For real!» Kimmy grinned.

«Yey!» Ashley shouted and gave her best friend a big hug. «This is so cool! Oh, and please, please, Kimmy, can I be your campaign manager? I will make you win!»

«Of course,» Kimmy laughed, «I'd love you to be my campaign manager!»

«Yay!» Ashley said and hugged Kimmy again. «Got to go now,» she pointed to the group of cheerleaders that had already started practicing. «This is so cool. Kimmy for president!» she shouted as she jogged over to the other cheerleaders.

Kimmy smiled as she got her camera ready to take some photos of the girls. She was so excited about her plan. And with Ashley on her team, running for class president was going to be superfun.

Als Nico und Zach die Sportplätze erreichten, war dort schon einiges los. Auf einem weit hinten gelegenen Feld entdeckte Nico sogar schon ein paar Fußballspieler, die sich, wie es aussah, gerade warm liefen. Gut konnte er das allerdings nicht erkennen, denn die Sonne blendete mitten am Nachmittag sehr. Ein Haufen Fußbälle lag da am Spielfeldrand, das konnte er sehen, und in einem der Tore stand jemand, der definitiv Torwartkleidung trug.

Das sieht ja schon mal gar nicht schlecht aus, dachte Nico voller Vorfreude, während er in die Sonne blinzelte.

Am Rand eines näher gelegenen Feldes waren die Cheerleader schon mitten im Training. In kleinen Gruppen übten sie verschiedene Hebefiguren. Ganz vorne balancierten vier Mädchen ein fünftes auf ihren überkreuzten Armen und federten es, ähnlich wie auf einem Trampolin, hoch in die Luft. Das Mädchen sprang, machte hoch in der Luft einen Salto und landete kerzengerade auf den Armen der anderen. Nico war beeindruckt. Dass Cheerleader gut tanzen konnten, hatte er sich schon gedacht, aber solche Kunststücke hatte er nicht erwartet. Noch überraschter war er, als er das Mädchen erkannte, das schon wieder zu einem Salto in die Luft katapultiert wurde. Es war Ashley!

Auch auf dem Spielfeld, das direkt vor ihm lag, war unterdessen Bewegung entstanden. Eine große Gruppe breitschultriger Jungen, dick verpackt in eine noch breitere Schicht aus Schulterpolstern und allerlei anderer Schutzkleidung, lief sich brutal über den Haufen, um einen dunkelroten eiförmigen American-Football-Ball zu ergattern. Das war vielleicht ein Gerangel!

Typisch Amis, dachte Nico. Gerade wollte er Zach erzählen, dass er diesen Sport bisher nur aus dem Fernsehen kannte, da ergriff der schon das Wort.

«Cool, huh?», sagte er und deutete auf die vielen Sportlerinnen und Sportler um sie herum. «We're late. We better get changed. The locker room is over there.»

«OK», sagte Nico und folgte ihm in Richtung des Gebäudes, in dem die Umkleiden untergebracht waren. Doch dann blieb Zach plötzlich stehen.

«Got to talk to the coach first. I totally forgot», erklärte er. «You get dressed in there, I can change out here, I guess. Meet me on the field, OK?»

«OK», sagte Nico. Er blickte sich noch einmal um und sah, dass Ashley gerade wieder durch die Luft wirbelte. Allerdings kniete jetzt jemand vor der Cheerleadergruppe und fotografierte die Kunststücke. Diesmal erkannte Nico sofort, um wen es sich handelte, und auch das Mädchen mit dem Fotoapparat hatte ihn gleich entdeckt: Nico winkte, und Kimmy winkte zurück, bevor er im Umkleideraum verschwand.

Wenige Minuten später trat Nico wieder auf den Sportplatz. Er trug das Trikot seines Vereins in Deutschland, das mit den vielen Unterschriften, seine Stollenschuhe, Stutzen und natürlich Schienbeinschoner. Er freute sich so sehr auf das Fußballtraining, dass er es kaum abwarten konnte. Übermütig setzte er zum Joggen an und trabte schwungvoll am American-Football-Team vorbei in Richtung der Fußballtore.

«Nico?», hörte er plötzlich eine Stimme rufen.

Verdutzt sah er sich um. Doch außer den American-Football-Spielern war niemand in der Nähe. Hatte er sich verhört?

«Nico?», rief in dem Moment wieder jemand. Die Stimme schien tatsächlich aus der Gruppe vor ihm zu kommen.

Es war Zach, der aus der Gruppe der American-Football-Spieler heraustrat. Er trug die breiten Schulterpolster der American-Football-Spieler, unter den Arm hatte er einen Helm geklemmt.

Ungläubig starrte er Nico an.

Nico starrte zurück. Es schien ihm, als wäre es plötzlich ganz still geworden und als wären alle Augen auf ihn gerichtet.

«What the hell?», sagte Zach und musterte Nico vollkommen entgeistert.

Schlagartig war Nico klar, was passiert war. Und schlagartig wusste er auch, warum Zach so viel mehr nach Bodybuilder als nach Fußballer aussah.

«You play *American* football!», sagte er und trat einen Schritt auf Zach zu.

«Hell yeah, I play American football», antwortete Zach. Einige der anderen Spieler begannen zu lachen.

«I thought ...», versuchte Nico sich zu erklären, «that you played ... *normal* football!»

«What's this guy talking about?», fragte einer der Jungen.

«Did he just say ‹normal› football?», fragte ein anderer Spieler.

«This guy is crazy, man!», sagte ein anderer. Jetzt lachten wirklich alle.

Zach musterte immer noch völlig entsetzt Nicos Outfit.

«I thought ...», stammelte Nico und deutete hilflos auf den entfernt gelegenen Fußballplatz.

Plötzlich beendete eine laute Stimme das Lachen und Tuscheln auf dem Feld.

«Zach, is that the German boy you were talking about?» Der American-Football-Trainer war zu seinem Team hinzugetreten. Auch er musterte Nico verwundert. «Why on earth is he wearing a soccer uniform?»

Nico wäre am liebsten im Erdboden versunken, aber er versuchte tapfer zu bleiben.

«I didn't know you meant *American* football», versuchte er mit hochrotem Kopf zu erklären.

«Man! What other football is there?», fragte Zach. Wieder begannen die Spieler zu grinsen.

«Calm down», sagte der Trainer streng zu seinem Team. Doch Nico sah, dass auch er sich ein Lächeln nicht verkneifen konnte. «I know what's going on. This boy», er deutete auf Nico, «is from Europe. And in Europe, believe it or not, people call soccer ‹football›!»

Jetzt brüllten die American-Football-Spieler vor Lachen.

«Hey Zach! Our girls' soccer team is pretty good, maybe your German host brother wants to play with them», sagte ein besonders muskelbepackter Junge und haute Zach auf die Schulter.

«The girls?» Nico verstand gar nichts mehr.

«Soccer is for girls!» Mit einem Gesichtsausdruck, den Nico nicht deuten konnte, zeigte Zach auf das weit hinten gelegene Spielfeld.

Nico folgte seinem Blick. Und tatsächlich! Bei genauerem Hinsehen erkannte er es: Die Fußballspieler auf dem abseits liegenden Platz waren alles Spielerinnen. Es war ein Mädchenteam, das dort einen Ball nach dem anderen im Tor versenkte.

«He does look a little girly in that uniform», rief einer der American-Football-Spieler. «Come on, Euro-boy, why don't you go over there and play soccer with your girlfriends?»

Alle anderen brachen wieder in Gelächter aus. Nico sah, dass jetzt auch Zach grinste.

Das gab Nico den Rest. Vor lauter Wut und Scham unfähig, auch nur noch ein Wort zu erwidern, machte er auf dem Absatz kehrt und stürmte vom Sportgelände.

Chapter Ten –
Erste Hilfe

Kimmy, who had just finished taking pictures of the cheerleaders, watched the strange scene from the sidelines. She saw Nico come out of the locker room, dressed in what was clearly a soccer outfit. Kimmy was confused. Hadn't Nico said that he played football? Hadn't Ashley been happy that Zach finally had someone at home to talk about football with? Why on earth was Nico dressed like a soccer player now? Kimmy watched Nico talk to Zach and the other football players, and she heard the boys laugh. Then, Kimmy saw Nico storm off the football field. He looked really angry and confused. Kimmy couldn't help herself: She had to find out what was going on. Quickly, she put the camera in a bag and ran after the German boy. Maybe he needed her help!

«Nico!» She shouted, but he didn't seem to hear her. «Hey,» she called again, «Nico! Wait!»

Nico turned around and looked at her for a second, but didn't stop walking. His face was red and his eyes looked furious.

«Nico!» she shouted again and when she finally caught up to him, she grabbed his arm. «Stop!»

«What?» he asked sharply and yanked his arm away from hers. «Do you … do you want to laugh at me, too?»

«No, of course not,» Kimmy said quickly. «Why are you so mad? What happened?»

«Didn't you listen? Like everyone else?» Nico asked. He looked really, really angry.

«No, I didn't,» she said defensively. «Nico, what's going on?»

Nico took a deep breath. «Zach … he … he always said he played football. And I play football, too!»

Kimmy looked at him, not fully understanding what he was saying.

«They all laughed at me, because … I didn't know …» Kimmy could tell that his voice was quivering with anger. «Zach *doesn't* play football!» he shouted.

Now Kimmy didn't understand at all what Nico was saying.

«I mean,» Nico explained, «he plays *American* football! I play *normal* football! *Real* football!»

«Ooooooh,» Kimmy said, slowly understanding. «When you say ‹football› in Europe, you mean … soccer?»

«Yes,» Nico said, staring at the ground. He still looked mad and confused. «I'm such an idiot.» Then he added: «No, *they* are such idiots, all of them!»

«It was just a misunderstanding,» Kimmy tried to cheer him up.

«HA!» Nico said, sounding bitter. «Didn't you hear? Everybody laughed! It was … terrible!»

Kimmy knew that Nico was right. She really wanted to say something that would make him feel better.

«Is it true?» Nico asked before she could speak.

«Is what true?» Kimmy asked.

«That in America, only girls play …» he paused, «… soccer?»

«Noooo.» Kimmy said a little too quickly. «Not only girls. Boys play soccer, too. Well, sometimes.»

Nico looked at her quizzically.

«Nico,» she said, «soccer is the most popular sport for girls in the USA. And here at Jefferson High, there's only one soccer team. It's the girls soccer team.»

«Great,» Nico said sarcastically, «really great!» He turned around and started jogging away. «I have to go!» he called over his shoulder.

Kimmy, however, wasn't one to give up easily.

«Wait!» she said, «I'm coming with you.»

Erst als Nico endlich die Straße vor dem Schulgelände erreicht hatte, verlangsamte er seinen Schritt. Er hatte keine Ahnung, wohin er eigentlich gehen sollte, aber im Moment zählte nur eins: Hauptsache weg von der Schule, weg von Zach und seinen bescheuerten Freunden. Nico fluchte. Was bildeten sich diese blöden Amis überhaupt ein? So wie eben hatte ihn in seinem ganzen Leben noch niemand behandelt – und so dumm hatte er sich auch noch nie gefühlt. Woher sollte er bitte schön wissen, dass Football nicht gleich Football war? Und wieso sollte Fußball urplötzlich nur etwas für Mädchen sein? Nico verstand die Welt nicht mehr. Wütend trat er nach einem Ast, der auf den Gehweg gefallen war.

«Nico, come on!», hörte er eine Stimme hinter sich. «Wait!»

Diese Kimmy war wirklich hartnäckig. Er zögerte, doch dann blieb er stehen und drehte sich zu ihr.

«Where are you going anyway?», fragte sie, als sie nach ein paar Schritten zu ihm aufgeschlossen hatte.

«Don't know», sagte Nico knapp.

«Come on», sagte sie freundschaftlich, «I'll buy you a soda.»

Super, dachte Nico schlecht gelaunt, genau das, was ich jetzt brauche: noch so ein blödes Ami-Wort, das ich nicht kenne.

«A what?», sagte er deshalb unfreundlich.

«A soda, a soft drink, you know», erklärte sie, «a glass of coke, a sprite …»

«No!», antwortete Nico schroff. Kimmy stand einfach nur da und sah ihn an. Dann lächelte sie ein bisschen.

Obwohl er immer noch vor Wut schäumte, wusste Nico, dass Kimmy nun wirklich nichts dafür konnte, dass Zach und die andern American-Football-Spieler solche Idioten waren. Und gestern war sie ja auch wirklich richtig nett gewesen.

«Sorry», sagte er etwas betreten.

«How about that soda?», fragte sie und lächelte noch ein bisschen mehr.

«OK», antwortete Nico. Dann fiel ihm etwas ein, das seine Laune gleich wieder verdüsterte. «I can't go anywhere … looking like this!» Er deutete auf sein Fußballtrikot und die Stollenschuhe.

«Sure you can, you look … cute!», sagte Kimmy.

«Cute!» Nico wurde gleich wieder ärgerlich. «I don't want to look cute! Cute is … stupid!»

«OK», sie lachte, «I meant that as a compliment.» Vor lauter

Ärger bemerkte Nico gar nicht, dass Kimmy etwas verlegen geworden war. «You look … athletic!»

«Mmmpf», machte Nico nur und kickte wieder nach dem Ast, der jetzt am Straßenrand lag. Vor einer Stunde hätte er das noch nicht für möglich gehalten, aber jetzt wollte er auf gar keinen Fall von noch mehr Leuten in seinen Fußballklamotten gesehen werden.

«I have an idea», sagte Kimmy. «Let's go to the newspaper office. I'm a reporter for the Express, you know. We have drinks there and cookies. Let's go to the office and hang out there. No one will see you there, and you can get your street clothes from the locker room as soon as everybody else has gone home.»

Nico zuckte mit den Schultern. «OK», murmelte er.

«Cool.» Kimmy schien sich wirklich zu freuen. «Let's go!» Sie drehte um und steuerte wieder aufs Schulgebäude zu. Nico stapfte lustlos hinterher.

Inside the school building, Kimmy took Nico down a long flight of stairs. Although the sun was shining brightly, it was pitch dark down here. Kimmy switched on the lights, walked down a long corridor and held a door open for Nico.

«Welcome to the Express Newspaper Office!» she said with a big smile. Nico walked into the room and looked at all the brand new computers, printers and scanners that sat on the desks all over in the big room. He also looked at the comfortable armchairs and the shelves full of books and newspapers and magazines. From Nico's face, Kimmy could see that he was surprised. Maybe German schools didn't have their own newspapers?

«Nice office,» he said and nodded.

«What do you want to drink?» She pointed to all the soda cans that sat on one of the tables in the back of the room. «And what kind of cookies would you like? We have chocolate and double chocolate and crunchy walnut and …»

«I think … some coke, please,» Nico answered and plopped down in an armchair.

«No cookies?» Kimmy asked as she handed him a can of coke.

«No, thanks.» Nico shook his head.

Nico opened his coke and took a big drink. Then he leaned back in his chair, looking to Kimmy like he was, at last, feeling a little less angry and confused.

Kimmy sat down, too. She opened a box of walnut cookies and started munching on one. They didn't say anything for a while.

«Thank you,» Nico said, suddenly.

«For what?» Kimmy smiled.

«For … bringing me here,» he said and tried to smile back. Kimmy could tell that he was still upset.

«Don't worry about … what happened out there,» she said to make Nico feel better. «I'm sure everyone will have forgotten all about it by tomorrow.»

«I don't think so,» Nico said gloomily. «I think the American football players won't forget this so quickly. Everybody laughed!» He was starting to look angry again.

Kimmy felt sorry for him, and she knew that he was right.

«Maybe you could ... stay away from the football team for a while,» she suggested. «You don't have to play sports, you know. You could do something else in the afternoons!»

«But what should I do?» Nico asked. «All I want is to play football, I mean,» he laughed bitterly, «soccer!»

«I can't really help you with that, I guess,» she said. «But I think I have another idea.»

«Yeah?» Nico asked. Kimmy couldn't tell if he was interested or if he was only trying to be friendly.

«You could be on my campaign team!» she said, looking excited.

Nico looked like he didn't know what she meant. Or maybe he just didn't like her idea, Kimmy wasn't sure.

«You know, the campaign for the class president elections. I need a team to help me win! I need lots of great ideas and a good strategy and any help I can get, really,» she explained.

«OK,» Nico said, still not sounding very interested.

«Does that mean you're coming to our first meeting?» she asked. «It's going to be a lot of fun, really!»

«OK,» he repeated.

«Cool!» Kimmy smiled. She felt really happy. She was looking forward to spending more time with Nico.

«Mmmh.» Nico nodded. Then he changed the subject. He pointed to a life-sized cardboard cut-out of a man in a football outfit. He looked very impressive, and the cut-out was so realistic that he almost looked like a real person.

«Who's that?» he wanted to know.

«Walter Payton,» she said. «Or Sweetness. That's his nickname.»

«Walter Payton ... Sweetness ...» Nico looked like he was remembering something. «Who is he?»

«One of the best American football players that ever lived,» Kimmy said. «That cut-out belongs to the football team, they only stored it here because they redecorated the locker room in the summer, and they haven't come back for it yet.»

«And that Walter Payton ... is he famous?» he asked.

«He's very famous, and he's an idol for many players. Last year, actually, Zach played so well that the other football players started calling him ...»

«... Sweetness.» Nico finished her sentence. He sighed. «That must be what Zach meant when I talked to him earlier.»

Kimmy nodded. «Zach is Walter Payton's biggest fan. But really, everybody knows who Sweetness was, even people who are not football fans,» Kimmy explained.

«Everyone except me,» Nico said and looked upset again.

«Oh, come on, Nico,» Kimmy laughed, «you're not American! You've only been in the US for a few days. Don't be so hard on yourself!»

«Mmmmh,» he said again. This time, however, Kimmy could see that Nico was smiling back at her, at least a little bit.

Kapitel elf –

Nico likes …

Auch noch eine Woche später lief Nico vor Wut dunkelrot an, wenn er an den Nachmittag auf dem Sportplatz dachte. Zach hatte ihn seitdem ziemlich links liegen lassen. Er schien jetzt noch weniger zu wissen, was er zu Nico sagen sollte, und verdrückte sich, sobald Nico im Raum war. Und Ashley, na ja, die hatte ihn ja vorher schon ignoriert. Zu Hause bei den McMannons war Nico also meistens auf sich allein gestellt. Wenn er keine Schularbeiten machte – und davon gab es an der Jefferson High mehr als genug –, saß er alleine in seinem Zimmer. Er war ziemlich frustriert. So hatte er sich seine Zeit in Amerika wirklich nicht vorgestellt! Wenn er daran dachte, dass er vor seiner Abreise davon geträumt hatte, die Amis mit seinen Fußballkünsten zu beeindrucken, kam er sich richtig dumm vor. Er hatte sich wirklich vorgestellt, dass er sich mit Zach und den Jungs aus der Mannschaft anfreunden und jede freie Minute mit ihnen verbringen würde, genauso wie in Deutschland eben … Und jetzt, jetzt war das ganze Gegenteil passiert! Sobald er in der Schule den American-Football-Spielern und ihren vielen Freunden über den Weg lief, fing das Gelächter und Getuschel wieder an.

«Hey, Euro-boy! Where are your girlfriends?»

«European football – what a joke!»

«Is that the guy who didn't know what football is?»

Nico konnte es nicht mehr hören. Was sollte an American Football überhaupt so toll sein?, dachte Nico immer und immer wieder missmutig. Das war doch eigentlich nur eine Prügelei um einen seltsam aussehenden Ball – mit Sport hatte das, seiner Meinung nach, nicht viel zu tun, und mit Fußball – echtem Fußball! – konnte es schon gar nicht konkurrieren. Allerdings beneidete er die American-Football-Spieler an der Jefferson High auch ein bisschen. Sie waren regelrechte Stars an der Schule, und sie schienen eine wirklich erfolgreiche Mannschaft zu sein.

All diese Überlegungen änderten nichts daran, dass Nico ziemlich alleine war. Der einzige Lichtblick war in den letzten Tagen Kimmy gewesen: Immer, wenn sie sich in der Schule trafen, hatte er sich richtig gefreut – und ihr schien es genauso zu gehen. Nur diese Sache mit der Jahrgangssprecherwahl konnte er immer noch nicht verstehen. Was war daran schon besonders? Und wieso brauchte Kimmy ein ganzes Team von Wahlhelfern, wenn es nur darum ging, etwas so Langweiliges wie Jahrgangssprecherin zu werden? In seiner Schule in Deutschland waren die meisten Schüler froh gewesen, wenn sich überhaupt jemand freiwillig für dieses Amt gemeldet hatte!

Einerseits aus Verzweiflung über die Blamage auf dem Football-Platz, andererseits, weil er Kimmy einen Gefallen tun wollte, hatte Nico sich trotzdem bereit erklärt, beim Wahlkampf mitzumachen. Campaign team statt football team, dachte Nico etwas bedrückt, so hatte er sich das wirklich nicht vorgestellt! Er vermisste es schon jetzt, mit seinen Jungs über den Platz zu sprinten und den Ball mit Wucht in die Maschen zu jagen.

Wie auch immer, heute Nachmittag sollte das erste Treffen

des Wahlkampfteams stattfinden. Nico war auf dem Weg zum Büro des Express, denn dort trafen sich alle Helfer, die Kimmy organisieren konnte.

Helferinnen, verbesserte Nico sich in Gedanken, als er die Tür der Zeitungsredaktion öffnete: Das ganze Cheerleading Team war hier versammelt und dazu noch zahlreiche Mädchen aus seinem Jahrgang. In der Mitte des Raumes standen Kimmy und Ashley. Das gibt es nicht, durchzuckte es Nico, ich bin der einzige Junge hier!

«OK, people,» Kimmy shouted the moment she saw Nico enter the room, «let's begin!»

«Thanks for coming, everyone,» she continued, «and welcome to our first campaign team meeting.»

Kimmy smiled when all the girls started clapping and cheering. She saw that Nico didn't join in. Instead, she noticed, he looked around himself a little uncomfortably.

«My name is Kimmy Williams, but you all know that already, and I'm running for sophomore class president,» she went on.

The girls cheered even louder. Now, Kimmy noted happily, Nico clapped his hands, too.

«And this here,» Kimmy pointed to Ashley, «is my campaign manager, the wonderful Ashley McMannon!»

Everybody clapped and cheered again.

Then Ashley started talking. Kimmy looked at her best friend proudly. Ashley had thought of everything! She had thought of posters, flyers, speeches and lots of fun activities that needed to be organized by the campaign team. While Ashley divided all the helpers into groups, Kimmy found her way over to Nico, who was still standing at the back of the room near the door.

As exciting as all this was, all Kimmy wanted to do now was to go and talk to Nico. She had felt it the first time she had first seen him in front of the school, weeks ago, and she still felt it now: there really was something about that German boy. Kimmy couldn't explain, but she admitted to herself that she simply liked him a lot better than all other boys she had met. Right now was a perfect moment to get to know him even better and to find out if he might want to get to know her better, too!

«Hey,» she said to Nico.

«Hello,» he answered.

«So, thanks for coming,» she smiled and was happy to see that Nico gave her a smile, too.

Nico war mit voller Absicht bei der Tür stehen geblieben und hatte Ashleys Vortrag lieber mit etwas Abstand verfolgt. Mit diesen ganzen Mädchen Poster malen, Girlanden ausschneiden oder einen Kuchenverkauf organisieren – das klang in Nicos Ohren eher nach einer Strafe als nach allem anderen! Gerade in dem Moment, als er sich leise aus dem Raum schleichen wollte, war Kimmy neben ihm aufgetaucht. Nico wusste nicht, wie sie das immer wieder machte: Sie brauchte ihn nur anzulächeln, schon fühlte er sich um Klassen besser. Und irgendwie, fand Nico, sagte sie auch immer genau das Richtige.

«I'm really glad you showed up», erklärte sie gerade, «I was worried you might have other things to do.»

«What else should I be doing on a Tuesday afternoon?», versuchte Nico einen Witz. «Playing American football?»

«I guess not.» Kimmy lachte. «But you know, I'm really glad you're here, Nico», sagte sie und berührte dabei wie zufällig seinen Arm. Nico war selbst überrascht, als er merkte, wie sein Herz plötzlich schneller schlug.

«I'm … I'm glad, too», sagte er etwas stockend. Gerade fiel ihm das Englischsprechen wieder genauso schwer wie an seinen ersten Tagen in Charlotte. Kimmys Lächeln erschien ihm plötzlich noch strahlender.

«Does that mean, I mean», sie verhaspelte sich etwas, «does that mean I'll see you here every week now?» Nico bemerkte, dass Kimmy genauso klang, wie er sich fühlte: etwas verlegen – und ziemlich aufgeregt. «We're meeting every Tuesday and Thursday from three to six.»

Jetzt steckte Nico in einer Zwickmühle. Sechs Stunden in der Woche mit all diesen Mädchen im Campaign Team arbeiten – eine schrecklich langweilige Vorstellung. Andererseits bedeutete das aber auch zwei Nachmittage in Kimmys Nähe …

«I'd love to see you, you know», fügte sie mutig hinzu und sah ihm direkt in die Augen.

Jetzt gab es für Nico nichts mehr zu überlegen. «Of course I'll come», sagte er entschlossen – und mit etwas weichen Knien.

Als Nico am Abend zurück ins Haus der McMannons kam, war er fix und fertig. Es war ein langer Tag gewesen, und irgendwie war es total anstrengend, ständig Englisch sprechen zu müssen. Zu Hause hätte er sich jetzt mit seinen Kumpels getroffen und zum Entspannen ein bisschen gekickt – aber das, fiel Nico niedergeschlagen ein, ging ja leider nicht mehr.

Im Haus war es ruhig, auf den ersten Blick schien niemand da zu sein. Zach war sicher immer noch beim American-Football-Training, oder, dachte Nico etwas gehässig, er unternahm mit seinen ‹tollen› Freunden aus seiner ‹tollen› Mannschaft irgendetwas besonders ‹tolles› Amerikanisches. Ashley konnte auch nicht zu Hause sein, sie hatte noch mit den anderen Cheerleadern gelacht und geredet, als Nico das Express-Büro verlassen hatte.

Als er die Küche betrat, saß dort Mrs McMannon am Tisch und klappte gerade den Laptop zu.

«Hi there, dear», sagte sie in ihrem charmanten Tonfall, als Nico hereinkam.

«Hello», antwortete Nico.

«Listen honey, I have to go now», erklärte sie, während sie aufstand und eine Strickjacke von der Stuhllehne zog. «But I made dinner! It's in the fridge, and you can heat it up whenever you're hungry. Do you need anything else?»

«No, thank you, I don't think so», erwiderte Nico, dann fiel sein Blick auf den Computer und er sagte: «Oh! Maybe there is something.»

Mrs McMannon hielt inne. «What is it, dear? Is there anything I can do for you, honey? Anything at all?»

An ihre überfreundliche Art hatte Nico sich mittlerweile schon gewöhnt. «Could I use the laptop to check for new e-mails?»

«Oh, honey, absolutely! No problem at all!», antwortete Mrs McMannon und war damit auch schon aus der Tür verschwunden.

Also schnappte sich Nico den Laptop und öffnete sein E-Mail-Programm. Neben der üblichen Mail von seiner Mutter, die ihm fast jeden Tag schrieb, war eine Überraschung in seinem Postfach: eine Nachricht von seinem Fußball-Trainer aus Deutschland!

«Hallo, Fußball-Ass, was macht das Leben in Amerika?
Lass mal von Dir hören! Grüße von der ganzen Mannschaft,
Dein Coach»

Nico musste grinsen, doch gleichzeitig wurde er ganz schön wehmütig ... gerade jetzt vermisste er seine Freunde wirklich sehr! Was hätte er nicht für einen Abend mit seinen Jungs gegeben! Umso mehr freute er sich, dass seine Mannschaft ihn anscheinend noch nicht vergessen hatte. Er brannte darauf, ihnen seine Erlebnisse zu erzählen und etwas Dampf abzulassen. Also machte er sich gleich an eine Antwort und tippte, ohne groß zu überlegen, alles, was ihm durch den Kopf schoss, in die Tasten.

Hallo Coach, hallo Team,
Ihr könnt Euch nicht vorstellen, wie verrückt diese Amis sind!

Erinnert Ihr Euch daran, dass ich Euch erzählt habe, dass mein Gastbruder Fußball spielt? Ich hab mich gleich in der ersten Woche total blamiert, weil ich natürlich nicht wusste, dass er die ganze Zeit von *American Football* geredet hat! Angeblich ist unser Fußball nur was für Mädchen! Könnt Ihr das glauben? Total bescheuert! Seit ich hier bin, habe ich nicht einen Ball gekickt!
Noch unvorstellbarer: Statt Fußball bin ich in einem Wahlkampfteam für die Jahrgangssprecherwahlen. Das ist hier in den USA eine total große Sache. Kimmy, das ist das Mädchen, für die wir den Wahlkampf machen, hat auch die ganzen Cheerleader für die Kampagne eingespannt. Echt krass übrigens, was die für Kunststücke draufhaben! Aber ansonsten sind die Leute hier nicht so toll, wie man vielleicht denken könnte. Ich habe mir die Amis zumindest cooler vorgestellt. Nur Kimmy ist da ganz anders. Sie ist irgendwie die Einzige hier, die mich versteht.

Nico hörte auf zu tippen und blickte auf seine Mail. Er war selbst überrascht über diesen letzten Satz. Aber es stimmte: Kimmy war wirklich die einzige Person in Charlotte, mit der er sich richtig wohlfühlte. Seltsam, dass ihm das erst jetzt beim Schreiben so richtig aufgefallen war … Als er noch grübelte, hörte er, wie sich die Haustür öffnete. Das war sicher Ashley, die nach Hause kam. Nico wollte auf keinen Fall, dass sie sah, was er geschrieben hatte, auch wenn sie wahrscheinlich kein Wort verstanden hätte. Außerdem, beschloss er, war sein Geschreibsel über Kimmy mehr als peinlich. Auf keinen Fall konnte er die Mail so losschicken. Also löschte er schnell die letzten beiden Sätze und schrieb stattdessen:

Macht's gut, Euer Nico

Er schickte die Nachricht ab, klappte den Laptop zu und fühlte sich zumindest ein bisschen besser.

Chapter Twelve – ***Geheimnisse***

Ein paar Wochen später lief die Arbeit von Kimmys Wahlkampfteam auf Hochtouren. Jeden Dienstag und jeden Donnerstag trafen sich ihre Unterstützerinnen – und Nico – im Büro der Schülerzeitung, um die nächsten Schritte zu planen und anstehende Aktionen vorzubereiten. Anfangs war Nico einfach nur überrascht davon gewesen, wie viel es zu tun gab und wie viel Mühe das Team in die Arbeit steckte. Nach und nach merkte er allerdings, dass auch die Teams der Gegenkandidaten – zwei Jungen namens Devon und Rashid, die Nico nur vom Sehen kannte – mindestens genauso begeistert bei der Sache waren und alles daransetzten, die Ideen von Kimmys Team zu übertrumpfen. Nach wie vor war Nico nicht wirklich begeistert davon, ständig mit all den Mädchen zusammen zu sein, aber immerhin hatte er so zwei Nachmittage in der Woche etwas anderes zu tun, als alleine bei den McMannons herumzusitzen und das peinliche Schweigen zu ertragen, das immer dann entstand, wenn Zach ins Zimmer kam. Wenn Zach und Ashley sich nicht gerade vor ihm stritten, hörte er so gut wie nichts von seinen Gastgeschwistern. Der Hauptgrund dafür, dass Nico nach wie vor zu jedem Treffen des Campaign Team kam, waren aber natürlich nicht Ashley oder Zach.

«Nico!», hatte Kimmy beim letzten Treffen gestrahlt, als sie zur Tür hereingestürmt war. «I'm so glad you're here!»

Nico war vor Freude ein bisschen rot geworden. Ob Kimmy sich wohl nur freute, weil er als einziger Junge in ihrem Team mithalf – oder ob da noch mehr hinter ihrem Lächeln steckte? Nico hoffte es zumindest.

Heute war Kimmy noch nicht in der Wahlkampfzentrale aufgetaucht. Nico saß gerade mit einigen Cheerleadern an dem großen runden Tisch in der Mitte des Büros. Sie waren schon seit einiger Zeit damit beschäftigt, riesige Plakate zu beschriften und zu verzieren. «Kimmy for President» stand auf den meisten. Auf anderen war «Kimmy is the best!» oder «Sophomores need Kimmy Williams!» zu lesen. Die Arbeit war ziemlicher Kindergartenkram, fand Nico, und mit den Mädchen an seinem Tisch hatte er sich wenig zu sagen. Sie erinnerten ihn alle sehr an Ashley: Die ganze Zeit unterhielten sich nur über Cheerleading – über neue Tanzschritte und Hebefiguren und den nächsten großen Auftritt. Interesse für einen deutschen Austauschschüler schienen sie nicht gerade zu haben. Meistens blieb Nico nicht viel anderes übrig, als den Cheerleadern stumm bei ihren Gesprächen zuzuhören und ein nicht allzu gelangweiltes Gesicht zu machen.

Irgendwie, merkte Nico, konnte er den Mädchen ihr Verhalten nicht einmal übel nehmen. Zu Hause war er schließlich selbst nicht anders gewesen: Da hatte er auch am liebsten stundenlang mit seinen Kumpels über Fußball geredet: Fußball und nichts als Fußball! Wie sehr er das Kicken vermisste! Seit dem Zwischenfall mit dem American-Football-Team hatte er seine Stollenschuhe nicht mehr angefasst. Doch während er hier ein Plakat nach dem anderen beschriftete, begann er zu träumen. In seinen Gedanken stürmte er über das Spielfeld. Es gab nur ihn und den schwarz-weißen Lederball. Er spürte die anderen Spieler in seinem Rücken, und Adrenalin schoss durch seinen Körper, denn vor seinem inneren Auge sah er schon das gegnerische Tor …

«Nico! Hey!», wurde er von Kimmys Stimme aus seinem Tagtraum gerissen.

«Hi …», antwortete er überrascht. «I didn't hear you come in. I was … concentrating on the poster.»

«Oh, really?», fragte Kimmy grinsend mit einem Blick auf das Plakat, an dem er arbeitete.

Nico folgte ihrem Blick und sah, dass da ein völlig leeres Blatt vor ihm lag.

«Oh», sagte er.

Kimmys Augen funkelten, als sie weitersprach. «Looks to me like you were lost in a day-dream. Tell me, Nico, what were you dreaming?»

«Yeah, maybe I was!», gab er zu und lächelte. Er konnte es fast nicht glauben: Er flirtete mit Kimmy!

«So, what were you dreaming about?», hakte sie nach.

Das klingt jetzt sehr unromantisch, wenn ich die Wahrheit sage, dachte Nico bei sich. Aber lügen wollte er auch nicht. «It's a secret», sagte er deshalb. Dann setzte er noch einen drauf: «I'd like to tell you about it … but I have to get back to work! These posters are really important, you know!»

«Hhhm, interesting», sagte sie und lachte. «Maybe you can tell me about it later.»

«Maybe», sagte Nico. «Maybe I will. If you're nice!»

Kimmy was pleased with the campaign. Ashley had built up a great team and everybody was making a huge effort.

They had made posters all afternoon and now they were plastering the school walls with them. Kimmy and her best friend were alone in the Express office for the first time that day. They had been so busy campaigning that they had hardly had any time for a chat.

«Phew.» Kimmy sighed and dropped into a chair. «This is so much work. I've been so busy, I haven't had a free minute for weeks! What would I do without you, Ash?»

«I know!» Ashley sat down opposite her friend. She looked quite exhausted. «I'm so glad the cheerleading squad is helping us so much. And all the other girls!»

«And Nico, of course,» added Kimmy.

«Yeah, sure.» Ashley shrugged her shoulders. «I was actually wondering why …»

«Well, he was looking for something to do. So I asked him to help me with the campaign,» Kimmy explained quickly.

«Oh, really? That can't be all!» replied Ashley in a hushed, playful tone. «I think he … likes you!»

«What? Really? You think he likes me? Really?» Kimmy asked, sounding really excited. She noticed herself right away.

«Hang on!» Ashley's face lightened up and she sat up straight in her seat. «I only said that as a joke. But Kimmy! You like *him*! You like Nico, the German exchange student!»

«Well, yeah. He's a nice guy. Of course I like him,» Kimmy said defensively.

«No, no, no, girlfriend! You can't fool me!» Ashley laughed. «You officially have a crush on the German boy!»

Now Kimmy had to laugh, too.

«OK, OK, *maybe* a little bit …» she admitted.

«Ha! I knew it!» Kimmy shouted just as the door flew open and a bunch of cheerleaders and Nico came back into the room.

«You knew what, Ash?» asked one of the girls curiously. Nico looked over, interested, too.

«Nothing!» said Ashley and Kimmy at the same time.

«It's a secret.» Ashley added in a loud whisper and nudged Kimmy in the side, laughing, when she saw Nico's confused face.

Am Ende des Nachmittags, nachdem Kimmy vor ihrem Helferteam zur Probe eine Rede gehalten hatte, für die sie mit viel Applaus belohnt worden war, fasste Nico einen Entschluss. Was auch immer Kimmy und Ashley da gerade Geheimnisvolles zu besprechen hatten, änderte nichts daran, dass vorhin, als er mit ihr alleine geredet hatte, etwas zwischen ihm und Kimmy passiert war. Es hatte irgendwie geknistert, das hatte er genau gespürt. Also nahm er all seinen Mut zusammen.

«Do you want to do something with me on the weekend?», fragte er Kimmy, nachdem die anderen außer Hörweite waren.

«You mean», sie guckte etwas verlegen, «like a date?»

«Yes», antwortete Nico ebenso verlegen.

Kimmy zögerte bei ihrer Antwort keine Sekunde. «Yes!», erwiderte sie strahlend. «I'd love that!» Dann allerdings verdunkelte sich ihr Gesicht. «I have to write two articles for the Express on the weekend, and I have to practice my speech again, and there's so much homework … oh, and I have to babysit all day on Sunday …» Sie dachte ein paar Sekunden nach, dann aber lächelte sie wieder zuversichtlich. «If I get started on Friday, I'm sure I can finish everything by Saturday morning. And then I'll be free to see you by that afternoon! How does that sound?»

«Great!» Nico nickte zustimmend, und Kimmy redete begeistert weiter: «We could go for a walk, and then get some ice-cream! Oh, I know, I can show you my favorite café! How about … 3 o'clock at the McMannons? I'll pick you up!»

Nico fiel ein Ausdruck ein, den er mal von Zach gehört hatte, als der begeistert einem Vorschlag zugestimmt hatte. «Deal», sagte er und strahlte.

Kapitel dreizehn –

The busiest girl in the world

Am Samstag saß Nico mal wieder alleine im Wohnzimmer der McMannons. Endlich war ihm dabei einmal nicht langweilig, denn obwohl er wie so oft von einem Fernsehsender zum nächsten schaltete, wartete er gespannt darauf, dass es endlich an der Tür klingelte. In Gedanken sah er sich schon mit Kimmy in einem Café sitzen, mit Eis und mit jeder Menge zu reden und zu lachen … Vielleicht, dachte Nico mit klopfendem Herzen, guckt sie mich wieder so an wie beim letzten Mal … Jetzt war es Punkt drei! Kimmy musste also jeden Moment auftauchen! Und tatsächlich: Nico hörte Schritte vor der Haustür, dann eine Stimme … nein, es waren nur Mr und Mrs McMannon, die vom großen Wochenendeinkauf zurückkamen. Einen Augenblick später steckte Mrs McMannon den Kopf durch die Wohnzimmertür.

«Nico, darling, how are you?», sagte sie in ihrem immer charmanten Tonfall.

«I'm good», antwortete Nico, der sich mittlerweile an die amerikanische Art der Begrüßung gewöhnt hatte. «How are you?»

«Wonderful, just wonderful!», antwortete Mrs McMannon und setzte sich in einen der bequemen Sessel. «But tell me honey, didn't you say you were going out this afternoon?»

Nico merkte, wie seine Ohren ein bisschen rot wurden. «I'm waiting … for Kimmy», antwortete er schnell.

«Is that right?» Mrs McMannon war begeistert. «Kimmy is such a wonderful girl! She's very pretty, don't you agree, honey? Such a good student, too! She's a reporter for the school newspaper, and now she's running for class president … she is probably the busiest girl at Jefferson High!» Sie lachte.

Obwohl Mrs McMannon recht hatte, nickte er nur knapp. Dieses Gespräch war wirklich nicht nach seinem Geschmack, und er hätte lieber wieder alleine gewartet. Allerdings sah es nicht so aus, als ob Mrs McMannon es eilig hätte, ganz im Gegenteil. Es schien ganz so, als ob sie die Zeit nutzen wollte, sich endlich einmal ausführlich mit ihm zu unterhalten.

«So, Nico, dear», sagte sie, «how do you like your new life in the US? I sure hope everything is going just great for you, hon!»

Nico nickte wieder nur und lächelte höflich. Schließlich konnte er Mrs McMannon ja nicht erzählen, dass er – wenn man mal von Kimmy absah – die letzten Wochen alles andere als großartig gefunden hatte. Und dass er die meiste Zeit damit zubrachte, sich nach Hause, nach Deutschland und auf den Fußballplatz zu wünschen, war sicher auch nicht das, was Mrs McMannon hören wollte.

«We want you to know, honey, that Bruce and I are more than happy to have you at our home», führte sie ihren Gedanken fort, «and we want you to know that you're part of the McMannon family just like everybody else at this house.»

Nico konnte sich den Gedanken nicht verkneifen, dass Zach und Ashley da sicherlich anderer Meinung waren. Vielleicht hatte Mrs McMannon das ja gerade auch nur gesagt, weil sie gemerkt hatte, dass zwischen Zach, Ashley und ihm – milde ausgedrückt – alles andere als familiäre Stimmung herrschte? Wie auch immer, beschloss Nico, es war wirklich nett von Mrs McMannon gemeint.

«Thank you», sagte er deshalb, «it's very nice of you … to let me stay at your house, and», fügte er etwas unbeholfen hinzu, «that you say that I'm … part of the family.»

Mrs McMannon lächelte. «We call it Southern hospitality, darling. Here in the South, we are always very happy to have guests, and it is very important for us to make them feel welcome.»

Nico nickte jetzt wieder nur. Wann kam Kimmy endlich?

«I come from a very old Southern family», fuhr Mrs McMannon fort und sah dabei richtig stolz aus, «and we are proud of our traditions, and Southern hospitality is the most important one.»

Nico nickte wieder und sah verstohlen auf seine Uhr. Fünf Minuten nach drei. Sein Herz klopfte. Kimmy kam sicher gleich. Nico bemerkte, dass Mrs McMannon ihn erwartungsvoll ansah. Er musste sich wohl doch an diesem Gespräch beteiligen.

«Is your family from Charlotte?», war die erstbeste Frage, die ihm einfiel.

Mrs McMannon lachte. «Oh, honey, no! My family is from New Orleans, in Louisiana, the most beautiful city in the world. Louisiana used to belong to France, did you know that?»

Nico schüttelte den Kopf. Dass die USA aus britischen Kolonien entstanden waren, daran erinnerte er sich aus dem Englischunterricht. Aber von französischen Gebieten hatte er noch nie gehört.

«Before I married Bruce», fuhr Mrs McMannon fast schon verträumt fort, «my last name was LaCoeur – that means ‹heart› in French, isn't it beautiful? June-Marie LaCoeur was my name as a girl in New Orleans.»

Irgendwie passte das zu Mrs McMannon und ihrer eleganten Art, fand Nico. Und auch in seinen Ohren klang der Name sehr französisch. Gab es nicht auch eine Stadt in Frankreich, die Orleans hieß? Nico nahm sich vor, das später mal in einem Atlas nachzugucken. Jetzt aber sah er erst mal wieder auf die Uhr. Schon fast zehn nach drei.

Plötzlich öffnete sich die Wohnzimmertür. Erwartungsvoll drehte Nico sich um, doch es war nur Mr McMannon, der sich, mit einem großen Becher Kaffee in der Hand, neben ihn auf das Sofa fallen ließ.

«There's our host son!», sagte er zur Begrüßung. «How are ya, Nic?»

«Good, how are you?», antwortete Nico automatisch und ganz wie ein echter Amerikaner.

«Nico is going on a date, isn't it wonderful?», mischte sich Mrs McMannon wieder ein.

«Well all right!», lachte Mr McMannon. «So who is the lucky lady?»

«Kimmy», sagte Nico verlegen.

«Ah, the great Kimmy Williams!», antwortete Mr McMannon. «How does she have time for dates between being a student, a reporter and hanging out with our daughter?»

«Don't forget, Bruce, honey», warf Mrs McMannon ein, «she's also running for sophomore class president!»

«It sounds like you're going on a date with the busiest girl in Charlotte!», lachte Mr McMannon.

«Yes», antwortete Nico mit einem etwas angestrengten Lächeln. Hoffentlich hören die beiden endlich damit auf, dachte Nico. Wieder sah er auf die Uhr. Jetzt war es schon fast Viertel nach drei. Wo blieb Kimmy nur?

«Anyway», setzte Mr McMannon nach einer Pause wieder an, «Zach told me you're not on the football team after all!»

Das Thema war auch nicht besser, dachte Nico bei sich. Erstaunlich war es aber schon, fand er, dass Mr McMannon ihn nicht schon viel früher darauf angesprochen hatte! Wahrscheinlich, dachte Nico gleich wieder etwas übellaunig, redet Zach wirklich so gut wie nie ein Wort mit irgendjemandem!

«There was … a misunderstanding», sagte er vage.

«What is there to misunderstand about football?», lachte Mr McMannon. «I think we can all agree on this, football is the best thing in the world!»

Jetzt musste er wohl oder übel die ganze blöde Geschichte noch einmal erzählen. Oder zumindest eine Kurzfassung.

«I'm not on the football team because I don't play football», sagte er. «I mean, I play football, but it's European football. Soccer.»

«Oh! Really!» Mr McMannon sah wirklich überrascht aus.

«Yes», antwortete Nico und fühlte sich plötzlich überraschend selbstbewusst. «And SOCCER is the best thing in the world.»

Mr McMannon sah jetzt erst richtig verwundert aus. Doch dann lachte er. «Well, I think we're going to have to agree to disagree on that one! You know, I do respect the German soccer tradition. But like I said, we're just a football family, and it's a football country», sagte er freundschaftlich.

Nico lächelte. Mr McMannon war wirklich in Ordnung. Gerade wollte er wieder auf die Uhr gucken, da klingelte das Telefon. Mrs McMannon nahm ab.

«McMannon residence», sagte sie. Dann schwieg sie, nickte und lächelte. «Oh hello, Kimmy! Yes dear, he's right here», sagte sie und reichte das Telefon an Nico weiter.

«I'm sooooo sorry, Nico», hörte er Kimmys Stimme, «but I won't be able to make it. I still have two articles to write, and I haven't done my Spanish homework, and there's so much stuff I need to get done!»

Nico konnte die Enttäuschung richtig im Magen spüren. «OK», brachte er nur heraus.

«I'll talk to you on Monday, OK?», sagte sie noch, da war das kurze Gespräch schon vorbei.

«Kimmy is too busy», erklärte er niedergeschlagen.

Mrs McMannon sah ihn mitleidig an.

«Well, I'm not surprised», versuchte Mr McMannon es dann mit einem Witz, «you're trying to date the busiest girl in the world!»

Chapter Fourteen –
BÄNG!!!!!!

The next day – Sunday – Zach and Ashley were in the living room. Both were sitting on the couch, both were watching TV, or trying to watch TV.

«Just give me the remote for a second,» Zach said, «I want to check the football scores.»

«No way,» Ashley protested, «my favorite show is on in a minute, I'm not going to let you change the channel.»

«Come on! This is important!» Zach tried to grab the remote control from his sister. Ashley screamed dramatically but didn't let go.

«You have a TV in your room!» she said, «and there's one in the kitchen! Go and watch your stupid football there!»

«They're too small.» Zach tried to grab the remote from his sister again.

«Too small to check the scores? Sure. Try the internet,» Ashley retorted.

«Ok, I just want to watch the highlights. It's like two minutes. This TV is the only one that's big enough to see all the details.»

«No, you're going to start watching a game and it's going to take three hours,» Ashley answered, «no way.»

«Just give it to me!» Zach insisted.

«No!» Ashley replied.

«Mooooom!» Zach shouted.

«Daaaaad!» Ashley countered.

After a little while, Mrs and Mr McMannon looked into the living room.

«What's going on?» Mr McMannon asked his children.

«Ashley won't let me watch the game!» he complained.

«You're such a crybaby,» Ashley said.

«Oh, you two, really!» Mr McMannon said, sounding a little angry. «You're acting like little children! You're almost adults – can't you act your ages?»

«Ashley, honey, Zach, my dear,» Mrs McMannon chimed in, «won't you try to be kinder to each other? We should all be getting along, don't you think? Even if it was only for the sake of our guest!»

Zach sighed. Ashley rolled her eyes.

«Where is Nico anyway?» Mr McMannon asked.

Zach shrugged.

«Don't know,» Ashley said, «don't really care.»

«That poor boy,» Mrs McMannon said, half smiling, half looking sad.

Neither Zach nor Ashley reacted. Instead, Zach leaned over to Ashley and quickly snatched the remote from her while her guard was down.

«Moooooom!» Ashley screetched. «Tell Zach to …»

«You two!» Mr McMannon said angrily, «what has gotten into you? Your mother is trying to talk to you about your host brother and you can't even listen to her for one second?»

«Sorry, Mom,» both said at the same time.

«So why is he such a ‹poor boy›?» Ashley said, trying to sound interested.

«He was supposed to go on a date with Kimmy yesterday, and she cancelled. He hasn't left his room since.» Mrs McMannon explained.

«Oh, that,» Ashley said. «You know Kimmy! I'm sure she didn't mean to do that, she's just *way* too busy.»

«Even before that happened, though, Nico seemed so … quiet! I don't think he's happy here at all,» Mrs McMannon said, and Mr McMannon nodded. «I just wish we could make him feel better, you know!»

«Can't you spend some time with him?» Mr McMannon asked Zach.

«I don't know,» Zach said vaguely, then added, like it explained anything, «he plays soccer, you know, not football!»

«I heard that,» Mr McMannon laughed, «but come on, Zach, that's not a reason not to spend time with him!»

«Don't know.» Zach shrugged. «I don't know what I could do with him. I just want to concentrate on football, you know!»

«Your football career *is* important,» Mr McMannon nodded.

«What about you, Ashley dear?» Mrs McMannon asked.

«Mmmmh?» Ashley hadn't been listening.

«Can't you spend some time with Nico?» Mrs McMannon asked.

«Oh, come on! Mom! Please,» Ashley answered. «*I* never asked for a host brother! *I* never wanted another boy to live at this house! Why do *I* have to spend more time with him?»

Mr and Mrs McMannon didn't respond right away.

«Besides,» Ashley continued, «I *am* already spending time

with Nico! Tuesdays and Thursdays, from 3 to 6, every week. There. Are you happy now?»

Mr and Mrs McMannon looked at their daughter quizzically.

«The campaign team, he's on Kimmy's campaign team,» she explained impatiently.

«There must be something this family can do for Nico that doesn't have to do with Kimmy!» Mr McMannon said impatiently. «Any ideas?»

«No.» Zach said as he started to flip channels looking for a football game.

«No,» Ashley repeated. «And now give me back the remote, Zach!»

Nico saß auf seinem Schreibtischstuhl und guckte aus dem Fenster. In seinem Zimmer gab es wenig zu tun, es eignete sich eigentlich nur zum Schularbeitenmachen oder Schlafen. Beides war nicht hilfreich dabei, einen Sonntagnachmittag weniger langweilig sein zu lassen. Nico war immer noch ziemlich traurig über Kimmys Absage am Vortag. Endlich war mal etwas Gutes passiert – da wandelte es sich gleich wieder zu etwas Schlechtem. Wahrscheinlich stimmte es ja, seufzte Nico, und Kimmy hatte einfach nur keine Zeit gehabt. Falls es das war, könnte er sich gleich morgen wieder mit ihr verabreden und die ganze Sache wäre nur halb so schlimm. Vielleicht, dachte er dann, war das aber nur eine Ausrede, weil sie sich doch nicht mit ihm treffen wollte! Und vielleicht, spann er diesen Gedanken weiter, hat Kimmy gar kein Interesse an mir … vielleicht ist sie nur wie Mrs McMannon und ist zu jedem supernett und superfreundlich … vielleicht hat es auch etwas mit dem Gespräch zu tun, das Kimmy und Ashley so plötzlich abgebrochen hatten, als er in den Raum gekommen war? Vielleicht war das Ganze auch mal wieder ein blödes Missverständnis! Wieder einmal war es ihm total peinlich, dass er sich seine Verabredung mit Kimmy in den buntesten Farben ausgemalt hatte – nur um dann den ganzen Nachmittag alleine herumzusitzen. Genau das Gleiche wie mit der Fußball-Sache, dachte er. Nichts klappt, wie ich es will!!

Er stand auf und schaute sich in seinem Zimmer um. Hätte ich doch wenigstens einen Computer hier, dachte er zum hundertsten Mal, dann könnte ich zumindest ins Internet! Sonst gab es in diesem Zimmer nur ein Regal mit Büchern und alten Zeitschriften. Alle langweilig, hatte Nico schon vor Wochen festgestellt. Dann war da noch der Kleiderschrank, in den er alle seine Sachen gestopft hatte. Ansonsten war der Schrank vollkommen leer. Hier gab es wirklich rein gar nichts zu tun! Er könnte natürlich ins Wohnzimmer gehen und etwas fernsehen, aber er hatte überhaupt keine Lust, einem der McMannons über den Weg zu laufen. Frustriert ließ er sich aufs Bett fallen und starrte an die Decke. Wenn er jetzt zu Hause wäre, in Deutschland, dann wüsste er ganz genau, was er machen würde. Er würde sich seinen Fußball schnappen und ihn gegen das Garagentor donnern. Ein gutes Training und gleichzeitig die beste Methode, Frust loszuwerden. Aber hier ging das ja leider nicht. Nico fluchte, dass er seinen Ball nicht mitgebracht hatte. Egal, ob hier angeblich nur von Mädchen Fußball gespielt wurde – er hätte jetzt alles darum gegeben, mit einem Ball nach draußen zu gehen und sich abzureagieren. Wieder guckte sich Nico in seinem Zimmer um. Dann entdeckte er doch etwas. Oben auf dem Kleiderschrank, ganz hinten, schien etwas zu liegen. Irgendetwas, das er bisher noch nicht gesehen hatte. Er stand auf und stellte sich auf sein Bett. Wenn er etwas hüpfte, konnte er es erkennen. Er stieg vom Bett, schob seinen Schreibtischstuhl an den Schrank und streckte sich, so weit er konnte. Erst berührte er das Ding nur mit den Fingerspitzen, doch dann konnte er es tatsächlich herunterangeln. Prüfend sah Nico an, was er in seinen Händen hielt: Es war ein dunkelroter American Football. Zweifelnd wog Nico ihn in seinen Händen. Ein komisches Ding, dachte er. Nicht mehr ganz neu, das sah er gleich, aber fest aufgepumpt und prall. Nico überlegte kurz. Einen echten Fußball würde er so schnell nicht in die Hände kriegen – er musste wohl oder übel mit diesem seltsamen Ei vorliebnehmen. Kurz entschlossen sprang er vom Stuhl und stürmte aus dem Zimmer. Schließlich gab es nicht nur in Deutschland Garagentore, an denen man seinen Frust auslassen konnte.

«Ashley, honey, Zach, dear,» Mrs McMannon tried again, «there must be something we can do for Nico, as a family!»

«Hhmmm,» Ashley said, not interested at all.

Zach didn't say anything.

«We decided to have Nico stay with us, now we have to make

sure that he has a good time here in America,» Mrs McMannon continued.

«Your mother is right,» Mr McMannon said. «Everybody think. What can you do to help your host brother have a better time?»

«Don't know,» Ashley said.

Zach shrugged.

«Isn't there any activity that you kids could do together?» Mr McMannon asked.

Now both Ashley and Zach shrugged their shoulders.

«Come on, darlings,» Mrs McMannon said.

«I don't know!» Zach said.

«Don't ask *me*. *I* didn't want a host brother in the first place,» Ashley repeated.

Mrs McMannon sighed and looked at her husband for help. Just when Mr McMannon started to speak, there was an extremely loud sound outside.

BANG!!!!!

Ashley and Zach jumped in their seats.

Mrs McMannon shrieked and put a hand in front of her mouth. «Oh my goodness,» she said, «was that an explosion? Bruce, I told you to check those gas lines!»

BANG!!!!!

There the sound was again.

The four McMannons looked at each other.

BANG!!!!!

«What on earth is going on?» Mr McMannon said and stepped to the window. He looked outside.

BANG!!!!!

Suddenly, Mr McMannon laughed. «Wow. You have to see this!» he said.

Everybody came over to the window and looked outside.

«My goodness, it's Nico!» Mrs McMannon exclaimed.

«With a football!» Zach said. His mouth had dropped open from surprise.

BANG!!!!!

«Wow,» even Ashley said, «he's really hammering it!»

«He is,» Zach nodded, surprised.

BANG!!!!!

«Man, he's actually *really* good with that thing.» Zach added, sounding impressed.

Mr McMannon nodded. «Who would have guessed that a soccer player could do that with a football!» he laughed. «Well, I guess they do know how to kick!»

Ashley walked back to the couch, and so did Mr and Mrs McMannon. Only Zach kept standing at the window, staring at Nico and the football.

BANG!!!!!

BANG!!!!!

«Man, Nico is so good with that ball!» he mumbled to himself. He stared outside a little longer. Then, he turned and faced his parents.

«I think I just had an idea», he said with a big grin.

«What is it, dear?» Mrs McMannon said.

«I think I know exactly what Nico can do to have a better time! Really, it's perfect!» he said excitedly.

«What is it?» Mrs McMannon asked again.

«I really got to go,» Zach said without answering his mother's question. «This is … big! I'll talk to you later!» He stormed out of the room and out of the house.

Kapitel fünfzehn – ***The best kicker in the world***

Am nächsten Morgen passierte etwas Ungewöhnliches. Noch bevor Nico sich aus dem Bett gequält hatte, klopfte es dreimal laut an seiner Tür. Nico öffnete die Augen. Was war denn nun los? Sonst weckten ihn die McMannons doch auch nie? Und wer konnte so früh am Tag schon etwas von ihm wollen? Er setzte sich auf die Bettkante und rief halb fragend, halb auffordernd «Come in?!». Die Tür öffnete sich, und zu Nicos Überraschung war es Zach, der den Raum betrat.

«Hey man, got a second?», sagte er.

«Umm hmm …», machte Nico. Er hatte keine Ahnung, was er mit dieser Aussage anfangen sollte. Außerdem war er noch ziemlich verschlafen.

«OK, man, I got to get going so I can't talk now», Zach schien in Eile zu sein, «but I can talk to you after school. I can tell you more there.»

«After school …? Why?», fragte Nico verdutzt.

«I'll explain later. Got to run. I'll meet you in front of your classroom, OK?» Damit war Zach auch schon aus der Tür. «See ya later, man!»

Nico war nun vollkommen verwirrt. So viel hatte er Zach in den ganzen letzten Wochen nicht sprechen gehört. Und er hatte richtig begeistert geklungen! Und nett! Was hatte das zu bedeuten?

Nico, der den ganzen Vormittag über Zachs mysteriöse Ankündigung gegrübelt hatte, konnte den Schulschluss kaum erwarten. Als er nach seiner letzten Unterrichtsstunde die Klassenzimmertür öffnete, sah er Zach schon auf dem Gang warten. Nico kam die Situation unangenehm bekannt vor: Zach stand ungeduldig auf dem Gang, über seiner Schulter hing die überdimensional große Sporttasche, in der Hand hatte er einen Helm.

«Football?», fragte er Zach ungläubig und anstatt einer Begrüßung. Er konnte es kaum fassen. Seine Vorfreude und Aufregung waren plötzlich verschwunden.

«Football!», erwiderte Zach ebenso knapp, grinste aber dabei. «Come on!»

«No! I'm not going there!», sagte Nico energisch. «You know I don't play your football.» Er würde keinen Fuß mehr auf das Footballfeld setzen!

«Relax, man», entgegnete Zach gut gelaunt. «It's a surprise. I promise, you'll like it.»

«But …», begann Nico, doch Zach ließ sich auf keine Diskussion ein.

«No ‹buts›!», sagte er bestimmt und packte er seinen Gastbruder am Arm. Zielsicher dirigierte er ihn in Richtung der Sportplätze.

Wie immer waren viele der Felder besetzt. Ein Team großgewachsener Jungen trainierte Basketball. Weiter hinten sah Nico einige Mädchen mit Hockeyschlägern, und auch die Fußballtore standen wieder unter Dauerbeschuss. Misstrauisch schaute er Zach an.

«Zach! Tell me what's going on!», verlangte er. Er hatte keine Lust auf Überraschungen, jedenfalls auf keine, die mit Football zu tun hatten.

«Trust me, man!», entgegnete Zach und bugsierte Nico geradewegs auf das Footballfeld zu. Wie bei seinem ersten Besuch auf dem Sportplatz hatte sich dort bereits das Team versammelt. Dick in ihre Schutzkleidung verpackt, liefen sich die massigen Jungen warm oder warfen den eiförmigen Ball hin und her. Zwischen ihnen stand der Coach, der nun auf Zach und seinen unfreiwilligen Begleiter aufmerksam wurde.

«Hey, Zach», sagte er, als er auf sie zukam, und klopfte Zach auf die Schulter. «Hi», wandte er sich dann tatsächlich auch an Nico, «how have you been?»

Auch ein paar andere Spieler kamen nun zu ihnen und begrüßten die beiden.

«OK», antwortete Nico zögerlich. Es war ihm nicht gerade angenehm, wieder bei den Footballern zu sein. Auch wenn heute alle plötzlich richtig nett wirkten. Wo waren die dummen Sprüche über Fußball? Und seit wann interessierte sich hier jemand dafür, wie es ihm ging?

Zach schnappte sich in diesem Moment einen Football von einem seiner Mitspieler und warf ihn Nico zu, der den Ball aus Reflex fing.

«Show them!», forderte Zach Nico auf.

«Show them what?» Nico hatte keine Ahnung, was Zach von ihm wollte. Ob sein Gastbruder und die anderen sich einen Scherz mit ihm ausgedacht hatten?

«Show them how you kick, man!», erklärte Zach und grinste stolz in die Runde. «You'll see, guys, he's the best kicker in the world!»

Kicker?! Wenn Nico eben schon etwas verwirrt war, verstand er jetzt gar nichts mehr. «Zach!», fuhr er seinen Gastbruder ärgerlich an. «Stop it! I don't understand what's going on! Since when are you interested if I can kick? This is not soccer, remember?»

Trotz Nicos Wutausbruch blieb Zach die Ruhe selbst. «It's easy, man», erklärte er. «Our team needs a new kicker! Our old kicker finished school last year. I saw you kick that ball last night – and man, you're really good!»

Nicos Ärger war plötzlich verflogen. «There are *kickers* in American football? Like in soccer?», fragte er verdutzt.

«Seriously, have you ever *watched* a football game?», fragte Zach, aber er lachte dabei.

Nico schüttelte den Kopf.

«Kicker is big position in American football», schaltete der Coach sich ein. «They're needed to kick the ball at several important moments during the game, to score or move the ball down the field. We need a guy who can kick hard and accurate and do it all under pressure. A soccer player might be just what we're looking for.»

«Show the coach your kick, Nico!», sagte Zach.

«Hang on», hielt ihn der Trainer zurück. «First Nico will have to put on his gear.»

Mit diesem Satz deutete er auf einen riesigen Haufen an Ausrüstung, der ganz in der Nähe lag.

«You want me to wear that … to kick a ball?», fragte Nico immer noch etwas zögerlich.

«That's right. See you in a minute», sagte der Coach und gab ihm einen Klaps auf die Schulter, der so heftig war, dass er Nico gleich ein paar Schritte in Richtung der Umkleidekabinen beförderte.

Es dauerte einige Minuten, bis Nico die komplette Ausrüstung angelegt hatte. Als er endlich fertig war und in den Spiegel blickte, erkannte er sich kaum wieder. Er sah mindestens 20 Kilo schwerer aus und hatte auf einmal ein Kreuz wie ein Schrank. Niemals hätte er es für möglich gehalten, dass er durch ein paar Schoner und Polster so eindrucksvoll wirken könnte!

Ich seh aus wie ein echter Footballer!, dachte Nico verwundert. Er klemmte den Helm unter seinen Arm und joggte zum Feld.

Der Trainer erwartete ihn bereits, und auch das Team scharte sich zu einer Gruppe zusammen, als Nico angelaufen kam.

«Looking good, man!», rief jemand, doch diesmal hatte

Nico nicht das Gefühl, dass die Jungen sich über ihn lustig machten.

Langsam, aber sicher wurde Nico richtig aufgeregt. In seiner neuen Uniform fühlte er sich schon fast wie ein Footballer – jetzt musste er beweisen, was er draufhatte!

Der Coach erklärte ihm seine Aufgabe: «D'you see that target wall over there?»

Nicos Blick folgte dem ausgestreckten Arm des Trainers, und er erkannte eine Art Torwand. In ihrer Mitte befand sich ein gut sichtbares Loch.

«I need you to kick that ball right through that hole», sagte der Trainer.

Oh Mann, dachte Nico. Die Größe der Öffnung war nicht das Problem – aber die Entfernung! Das war alles andere als einfach. Noch dazu mit diesem Ball, mit dem er erst seit gestern ein bisschen vertraut war.

Aller Augen waren auf Nico gerichtet. Er nickte konzentriert. Jetzt würde sich zeigen, ob es sich gelohnt hatte, dass er sein ganzes bisheriges Leben auf dem Fußballplatz verbracht hatte.

«Let's go!», rief der Coach und passte ihm mit einem harten Wurf den Ball zu.

Nico fing den Football und drehte ihn in seinen Händen, um seine Nerven zu beruhigen. Sein Puls raste. Er positionierte den Ball sorgfältig auf dem Rasen und trat einige Schritte zurück.

Jetzt oder nie!, dachte er und visierte das Ziel an. Er fühlte, wie das Adrenalin durch seinen Körper rauschte.

Dann nahm er einen kurzen Anlauf, sprintete nach vorn

und traf den Ball mit der rechten Fußinnenseite. BÄNG!! Mit voller Kraft zog er das Bein durch, jeder Muskel in seinem Körper war angespannt, den Blick hatte er konzentriert auf die Torwand gerichtet.

Alle schauten wie gebannt dem Ball hinterher.

Er fliegt zu hoch!, fuhr es Nico durch den Kopf.

Doch genau in diesem Moment begann der Football sich abzusenken. Nico hielt die Luft an.

WOOOOOSH! Wie eine Rakete ging der Ball zu Boden und landete haargenau im Loch der Torwand.

Versenkt!, dachte Nico und riss die Arme in die Höhe.

In diesem Augenblick stürzten auch schon die anderen Spieler auf ihn zu.

«Nice job, man!», rief jemand.

«How did he *do* that?», fragte ein anderer bewundernd.

«I knew it!», rief Zach und stürmte auf Nico zu. «High five!» Nico schlug mit ihm ein.

So stolz war Nico seit langem nicht gewesen.

Von hinten drängelte sich der Coach durch die Menge der Footballspieler.

«Perfect kick, Nico, just perfect.» Auch er klatschte mit ihm ab. «You're very talented. And I can tell that you've played soccer for a while!»

«All my life!», antwortete Nico.

Der Coach nickte bedächtig und musterte Nico von oben bis unten.

«Are you willing to work hard?», fragte er. «Are you a team player?»

«Yes», sagte Nico, ohne zu zögern.

Der Coach nickte wieder. Dann klopfte er ihm auf die Schulter. Nico kippte fast aus seinen Schuhen, als er weitersprach.

«You're on the team! You're the new kicker!» Die anderen Spieler klatschten.

Nico starrte den Mann ungläubig an. Träumte er?

Der Coach wandte sich zum Gehen. Über die Schulter fügte er noch wie nebenbei hinzu: «Oh, before I forget, your first game is next week.»

Chapter Sixteen – **Ashleys Idee**

Als Nico am nächsten Morgen die Schule betrat, fühlte er sich wie ein neuer Mensch. Er war den ganzen Weg mit Zach gegangen, was noch nie vorher passiert war, und die beiden hatten sich ausgelassen unterhalten, was Nico fast genauso unglaublich vorkam. Auf dem Weg hatten sie schon einige der anderen Footballer getroffen, und auch sie waren wie ausgewechselt: Statt der dummen Sprüche über seinen Auftritt in Fußballklamotten hatten alle ihn genauso freudig begrüßt wie Zach.

«What's up, Nico!»

«Hey, Nico, great kick yesterday!»

«Welcome to the team, man!»

Nico konnte es noch gar nicht fassen. Endlich schien alles so zu laufen, wie er es sich gewünscht hatte: Er hatte endlich neue Kumpels, Jungs, mit denen er seine Freizeit verbringen konnte! Und er konnte wieder spielen, wenn auch nicht Fußball, dann aber einen Sport, den er jetzt, als offizieller Kicker der Footballmannschaft, richtig cool zu finden begann. Und schon in der nächsten Woche war sein erster offizieller Einsatz! Es war einfach unglaublich.

Fast hätte er Kimmy übersehen, die am Eingangstor der Schule stand. Sie hat gar keinen Schimmer, was sich seit gestern alles für mich verändert hat, schoss es ihm durch den Kopf.

Ihr schien auch gar nicht aufzufallen, dass er mit Zach unterwegs war. Wahrscheinlich war sie zu sehr in ihre eigenen Gedanken vertieft, dachte er. Oder es interessiert sie einfach gar nicht! Tatsächlich schien Kimmy Zach gar nicht wahrzunehmen, sie stürmte auf Nico zu und ließ sofort einen Wortregen auf ihn niederprasseln:

«Hi Nico, so glad you're here!», sagte sie aufgeregt und voller Tatendrang. «Sorry again about Saturday, but – I had the best idea! You want to hear it? See, I want you to do a speech with me – you know – me and the international student! I think that could be really fun – and I think everyone could identify with us! I mean, we're girl and boy, black and white, American and European – I think that would be really cool!» Nico guckte sie etwas verwirrt an. Gerade war er noch so konzentriert auf Zach und Football gewesen, und was wollte jetzt Kimmy alles von ihm? Er verfluchte insgeheim seine immer noch zu dürftigen Sprachkenntnisse. Um dem Tempo folgen zu können, das Kimmy da gerade an den Tag legte, reichten sie zumindest nicht aus.

So stammelte er erst mal nur «What??».

Kimmy wiederholte ihre aufgeregte Ansprache, diesmal zumindest ein bisschen langsamer, sodass Nico wirklich alles verstand. Was er antworten sollte, wusste er allerdings noch lange nicht. Nico zögerte. Er suchte verzweifelt nach einer schnellen Antwort, die auch noch ein bisschen diplomatisch war. Wenn er ganz ehrlich war, wollte er keine Rede halten, nicht einmal mit Kimmy. Außerdem lagen die Trainingsstunden der Footballmannschaft genau zeitgleich mit den Treffen des Wahlkampfteams, auch da konnte er also nicht mehr dabei sein. Nico war eigentlich erleichtert, dass er jetzt eine gute Ausrede hatte, bei diesem Mädchenkram nicht mehr mitzumachen. Wie er das Ganze Kimmy mitteilen sollte, ohne dass sie enttäuscht war, und wie er sie vielleicht gleichzeitig auch noch nach einer neuen Verabredung fragen sollte, war jetzt das Problem.

Während er noch überlegte, hörte er Zach das Wort ergreifen. Ziemlich von oben herab klang er dabei. «The thing is, Nico can't come to your meetings anymore. He's on the football team now. No more time for the girls' little project, isn't that right, man!» Er lachte und haute Nico auf die Schulter.

Nico sah Entsetzen in Kimmys Gesicht aufsteigen. Richtig verletzt sah sie aus. Nico stand immer noch nur da und wusste jetzt erst recht nicht mehr, wie er die Situation retten könnte.

Ohne ein Wort sah Kimmy Nico direkt in die Augen. «I'm sorry», war alles, was er rausbrachte, bevor er verlegen zu Boden guckte. Innerlich beschimpfte er sich gleichzeitig als Volltrottel. Warum fiel ihm jetzt absolut nichts ein? Er hatte doch mit Kimmy reden, sie überzeugen wollen, dass sie gute

Freunde – und vielleicht sogar mehr – waren, Wahlkampf und Football hin oder her!

«I'm sorry, too», hörte er sie noch flüstern.

Als er den Blick wieder hob, sah er Kimmy schon am anderen Ende des Flures davonstürmen. Sogar von hinten sah sie tief getroffen aus. Zu gerne wäre Nico ihr nachgerannt und hätte richtig mit ihr geredet – sicher hätte sie ihn verstanden! Aber da ergriff Zach schon wieder das Wort.

«She's my sister's friend», sagte er abfällig, «what can you expect?»

Als er Nicos betroffenes Gesicht sah, änderte er seinen Tonfall. «Come on, man», sagte er aufmunternd, «forget the girl! Think of our team, man, you're a football player now, a *real* Jefferson patriot!»

Nico nickte nur etwas lahm.

«All the football players eat lunch together. We'll see you at the cafeteria», sagte Zach noch grinsend und ließ Nico dann stehen.

Nico seufzte. Er wusste einfach nicht mehr, was er denken sollte. Endlich hatte er Freunde! Endlich konnte er wieder trainieren! Aber gerade jetzt war ihm erst richtig klar geworden, dass ihm etwas ganz anderes genauso wichtig geworden war: Kimmy. Sein Herz zog sich zusammen, wenn er an ihren traurigen Gesichtsausdruck dachte. Warum hatte Zach sich auch so arrogant und unfreundlich verhalten? Und warum hatte er selbst sich so unglaublich doof anstellen müssen?

Für den Moment, beschloss Nico, blieb ihm nichts anderes übrig, als abzuwarten. Mit Kimmy hatte er heute keinen Unterricht, und Zach würde er in der Cafeteria sehen. Wieder fiel ihm auf, wie hin und her gerissen er war. Denn trotz seines richtig schlechten Gefühls Kimmy gegenüber merkte er, wie sehr er sich freute, dass er nachher zusammen mit den Jungs Mittag essen würde. Bisher hatte er um den Tisch mit Footballern, der ganz in der Mitte des Raumes stand, immer einen weiten Bogen gemacht. Aber jetzt gehörte er dazu! Jetzt war er, Nico, einer der coolsten Jungs der Schule! Nico fühlte sich aufgeregt und stolz. Trotz allem – Kimmy zu verletzen war das Letzte, was er gewollt hatte. Grübelnd stapfte er in Richtung Klassenzimmer. Warum musste alles so kompliziert sein?

Kimmy didn't know if she was furious or sad. She stormed to the Express office, the only place where she knew she could be alone. She didn't have class for another hour, and no other student would come early in the morning if they didn't have class. She opened the door to the office, glad to have escaped everybody – and found someone sitting at one of the desks. It was Ashley. She was chewing on the end of a pencil, concentrating on something really hard. Ashley looked up and saw immediately that something was wrong. She jumped out of her seat and put her arms around her best friend. Kimmy started to cry. Between sobs, she told Ashley what had happened.

«He's friends with my brother now,» was Ashleys first response. «What do you expect?»

«But Nico …» Kimmy tried, «I thought he was … different! I really liked him …»

Ashley shrugged her shoulders. «He's just another football player now, just like Zach. All he's going to care about from now on is football.»

None of this would have happened, Kimmy thought to herself, if I hadn't been so busy. If I had had more free time, I wouldn't have needed to cancel my date with Nico on Saturday. Things would be totally different today, if I had been able to spend time with Nico – alone!

«I wish I had had the time to see Nico on Saturday,» she said quietly. «Maybe we'd still be friends, then.»

«Or more than friends,» Ashley laughed. «Is that what you're saying?»

«Too late now,» Kimmy said and felt like crying again. She also felt really angry. Angry at Zach, for being so arrogant. Angry at Nico, for letting her down. Angry at herself, for never having any time.

«I wish I had never started this stupid campaign,» she said and flopped down in one of the chairs. «I'm never going to win. I'm never going to be class president! This is a waste of my time, and your time, too, Ash!»

«You're not wasting your time!» Ashley said as she sat down on the armrest of Kimmy's chair. «I'm your campaign manager, remember? That means you're going to win!»

Kimmy rested her head in her hands. After a few seconds, she looked up at her best friend. «What are you doing here anyway? Don't you have class?»

Ashley smiled her famous smile. «Technically, yes. But I told Mrs Martinez I felt sick and needed some fresh air.»

«And she just let you go? You look totally healthy!» Kimmy said.

«Of course she did,» Ashley said proudly. «There's something more important going on, that's why I'm here.The other candidates have been having some great ideas. We need to make our strategy even better! That's why I called all the girls to an emergency meeting. Well, all the girls who don't have class right now,» she added when she saw Kimmy's worried face.

«Without telling me?» Kimmy asked. «I'm the candidate, remember?»

«I'm the manager, remember?» Ashley smiled.

«OK,» Kimmy said weakly.

At this moment, the door burst open. At least 15 girls walked into the room. Everybody was laughing and chatting. They all sat down, looking at Kimmy and Ashley expectantly.

Kimmy stayed in her seat, she was just not motivated. Ashley, on the other hand, jumped up.

«Welcome once again, everyone, thanks for coming this early in the morning. The two other campaign teams have had some really successful ideas: Devon and Rashid are doing much too well for us to be comfortable in this campaign. We need to think! We need new ideas! We need to make sure that Kimmy wins!»

The girls applauded.

«Let's brainstorm, people! Let's think of ideas!» she continued.

The girls started talking to their neighbors excitedly.

«Oh, and there's some news,» Ashley added. «From now on, we're a girls-only-team. No more boys, just us girls.»

Kimmy felt really bad again.

«Any ideas?» Ashley shouted after a few minutes.

«If we are all girls, how about a campaign only for girls?» somebody suggested.

«The other two candidates are boys,» another girl added, «it would make sense to make Kimmy a candidate for us girls!»

Kimmy didn't think it was such a great idea. She remembered her idea to do a speech with Nico, to reach girls *and* boys that way. She felt too miserable to speak up. Ashley, on the other hand, seemed very excited.

«Are we enough girls in sophomore year to win, without getting any votes from boys?» somebody else asked.

«Kimmy, what are the numbers?» Ashley asked.

As always, Kimmy was well informed. «There are 55 percent girls, 45 percent boys in sophomore year,» she explained with a sigh.

«That's enough! We can win without the boys!» somebody shouted.

Kimmy still wasn't too sure, but everybody else laughed and applauded.

«Let's try it, then!» Ashley said. «Let's try to reach all the girls in sophomore year! Let's make Kimmy class president!»

«Kimmy! Kimmy! We love Kimmy!» some of the cheerleaders shouted and did a little dance. The other girls clapped their hands.

Now even Kimmy had to smile. It *was* really nice to have all these girls support her. And it was absolutely amazing, Kimmy thought, that Ashley was helping her out so much.

«OK everyone,» Ashley said and took up her pencil and a piece of paper. «Let's collect some ideas. What do all the girls in sophomore year like?»

«We like Kimmy! We love Kimmy!» The cheerleaders cheered again. Everybody laughed.

«OK,» Ashley said and wrote down the words ‹Kimmy› and ‹love›. «What else?»

«Jeff High!» somebody shouted. «We love being Jefferson Patriots!»

«Romance!»

«Secrets!»

«Cool things!»

«Creativity!»

Everybody laughed again. Ashley wrote down these words, too. Then she looked at her notes. To Kimmy's surprise, she then said:

«OK, everyone, thanks for coming! We'll meet again at our usual time, and we'll talk about these ideas some more!»

All the girls filed out of the room, still talking to each other excitedly.

Ashley sat down at the table and looked at her notes again.

Kimmy – love – romance – Jeff. High – secrets – cool – creative

«I just had a fantastic idea,» she grinned.

«What is it?» Kimmy wanted to know.

«Didn't you hear all the girls' ideas?» Ashley smiled. «It's a secret! But I can promise you this much: It will get everybody's attention! And all girls are going to love it!»

«Oh, come on,» Kimmy said. «You are going to tell me! This is all about me and my campaign!»

«Yeah,» Ashley nodded, «you're right.» Kimmy sat down next to Ashley, and Ashley explained her idea.

«But isn't that … illegal?» Kimmy asked.

«I wouldn't call it that …» Ashley said. «I would call it cool and creative! Oh, and it's romantic, too!»

Kimmy thought Ashley's idea was great – but she was still worried. «I do think it's illegal,» she repeated.

«Don't worry,» Ashley said. «I don't want trouble either. I'll talk to Principal Monroe right now! He thinks the class president elections are super important. And you know how he always wants us to be creative? He's going to love the idea!»

Kimmy looked at her friend quizzically.

Then, Ashley explained to her just how she was going to convince the principal. «That way,» she ended, «it's going to *look* illegal, but it won't be illegal at all!»

«Great,» Kimmy nodded. She was starting to feel excited about Ashley's plan. It really was a fantastic idea for her campaign, and it was different from all other ideas Kimmy had heard. It really was cool and secretive and romantic! And, in a creative way, it was about Jefferson High and about herself!

«I'll do it right away, during lunch! Everybody will be in the cafeteria, nobody will see me,» Ashley said happily.

«OK,» Kimmy said. She was smiling, too.

«You'll see,» Ashley said, «this idea is amazing! Everybody will talk about it! The sophomore girls are going to love it. It's going to make you class president!»

Kimmy laughed and hugged her best friend.

Kapitel siebzehn – **Kimmy loves …**

Als Nico am Nachmittag aus der Schule trat, hatte er einen Entschluss gefasst. Sosehr er insgeheim erleichtert war, dass er nicht mehr mit den Mädchen Poster bemalen und Kuchenverkäufe organisieren musste, hatte er sich doch ganz schön mies gefühlt, als er Kimmy gestern gesagt hatte, dass er nicht mehr im Wahlkampfteam sein wollte, dass er jetzt – unglaublich, aber wahr – zur Footballmannschaft gehörte. Oder eher, dachte Nico, als *Zach* ihr das alles gesagt hatte. Ich hätte lieber alleine mit ihr reden sollen, überlegte er wieder. Ihren Gesichtsausdruck hatte er immer noch vor seinem inneren Auge. Überrumpelt hatte sie ausgesehen und ziemlich traurig. Das muss ich irgendwie wiedergutmachen, dachte er. Schließlich war es Kimmy gewesen, die ihm durch die letzten Wochen geholfen hatte. Und wer weiß, was jetzt zwischen uns wäre, dachte er, wenn sie unsere Verabredung am Samstag nicht abgesagt hätte … Vielleicht war ja doch noch nicht alles zu spät? Vielleicht würden er und Kimmy doch noch … Gleich kribbelte es ihm wieder so komisch im Magen. Sofort morgen früh wollte er sie auf dem Weg zum Erdkunderaum abfangen.

Auf dem Hof vor der Schule blieb er verwundert stehen. Eine große Traube von Schülerinnen und Schülern hatte sich hier versammelt, sie lachten und tuschelten. Nico schaute sich um. Direkt neben dem Haupteingang prangte ein Graffiti, das vorhin noch nicht da gewesen war. Nico trat näher heran, jetzt konnte er besser sehen. Zwei kunstvoll verschlungene Herzen waren da abgebildet. Nico stockte vor Schreck kurz der Atem, als er sah, was in den Herzen stand.

Wer war Jeff? Seit wann war da etwas zwischen Kimmy und einem anderen Jungen? Wieso hatte er davon überhaupt nichts mitgekriegt? Nico fühlte sich ziemlich benommen und hatte Schwierigkeiten, einen klaren Gedanken zu fassen. Schon wieder war etwas schiefgelaufen! Er strengte sich an nachzudenken. Er hatte in den letzen Wochen keinen Jungen namens Jeff kennengelernt. Andererseits gab es allein in seinem Jahrgang tausend Leute – und in der ganzen High School viertausend –, gut möglich, dass es Dutzende von Jungen mit diesem Namen an der Schule gab. Nico betrachtete wieder die Liebeserklärung. Ernst schien es dieser Jeff mit Kimmy auf jeden Fall zu meinen, da war Nico sich sicher, sonst hätte er sicher nicht – für die ganze Menschheit sichtbar – ein solches Bild gesprüht. Oder hatte Kimmy das Graffiti gemacht? Irgendwie glaubte er das nicht. Vielleicht war Kimmy schon lange mit diesem Jeff zusammen – und vielleicht hatte Kimmy einfach keinen Grund gesehen, ihm, einem x-beliebigen Austauschschüler, von ihrem Privatleben zu erzählen. Vielleicht war dieser Jeff auch der Grund gewesen, dass sie die Verabredung am Samstag abgesagt hatte! Und vielleicht, schoss es Nico dann durch den Kopf, hatten Kimmy und Ashley beim letzten Wahlkampftreffen so geheimnisvoll über genau diesen Typen geflüstert! Aber wenn das alles so war, dachte er verwirrt, weshalb hatte Kimmy dann heute Morgen so verletzt reagiert?

Er warf noch einen Blick auf das Graffiti. Plötzlich durchschoss ihn ein ganz neuer Gedanke. Vielleicht war ja eine ganz andere Kimmy gemeint! Warum sollte es ausgerechnet die Kimmy sein, die ich kenne, dachte er, den Namen gab es doch sicher wie Sand am Meer. Jetzt fühlte er sich wieder etwas besser. Und zu seinem Entschluss war er auch zurückgekehrt: Er musste mit Kimmy sprechen. Er würde sie direkt fragen, ob sie etwas mit dieser Zeichnung zu tun hatte. Wenn sie nein sagt, dachte er und schöpfte neuen Mut, frage ich sie, ob sie mit mir unser Date nachholt, mit Eisessen in ihrem Lieblingscafé und allem Drum und Dran, jetzt sofort. Und wenn sie ja sagt – dann kann ich das Ganze wohl ein für alle Mal vergessen.

When Kimmy walked out of the school that day, she still felt pretty bad about Nico.

«Why do you think Nico is acting this way?» she had asked Ashley over and over again all day. «I thought he liked being on my campaign team. I thought he might like … me!»

Each time, Ashley had only shrugged her shoulder. «He's a football player now. He's like Zach – all he is going to care about is the football team and playing football and watching football and talking about football – do you need me to go on?»

«But Nico isn't like that,» Kimmy had tried again.

«They are *all* like that,» Ashley had answered.

Kimmy had only nodded sadly. She still didn't believe it. But then, Nico had left the campaign and was now, to her surprise, a football player. That wasn't a reason to not talk to him, though, right? Kimmy debated with herself. Maybe she had to just forget about the campaign for a moment and about football. Maybe she needed to talk to Nico in private, without Ashely or Zach around. She thought back to the day when Nico had asked her out on a date. It seemed unbelievable that only about a week had passed. If only I had had enough time on the weekend, she thought for the millionth time, if I only I had had enough time to go on the date with Nico!

But then, on the other hand, Kimmy also had a reason to feel really good. When she looked at the graffiti with all the other students, she couldn't help but smile. Ashley had done a fantastic job! It really looked like somebody was in love! It looked really cool – and creative! And it's even true, Kimmy thought to herself – I love Jeff – Jefferson High. Now the question is, she kept thinking, does Jeff High really love me? Will all the sophomore girls love this graffiti so much that they'll vote for me? Will I really become sophomore class president?

Kimmy was so lost in her thoughts that she didn't look where she was going. She bumped into somebody's backpack.

«Sorry,» Kimmy said.

The person with the backpack turned around – it was Nico.

«Uhhmm,» Nico said, sounding surprised by their sudden meeting. «Hello.»

«Hey,» Kimmy said.

Then they both said nothing.

Kimmy tried to think of something to say. She really wanted to do something to make things right. But what could she tell him? After all, it was Nico's fault that she was feeling so bad – he hadn't done anything wrong! Or had he? Kimmy felt confused.

To say something, anything at all, she said: «How are you?»

«OK,» Nico said.

Kimmy tried to smile. She wasn't sure, but she thought Nico had smiled back. At least a little.

Then, she noticed, it looked like Nico wanted to say something. He seemed to be looking for words.

«I … I have to ask you something,» he began and paused. Then he pointed to the graffiti.

Kimmy nodded. «What about the graffiti?» she asked.

«Is it … about you?» he asked.

Now Kimmy couldn't help but smile widely. «Yes!» she said happily, «isn't it fantastic?»

Nico looked as if someone had hit him in the face.

Kimmy stopped smiling. She didn't know what it was, but something had just gone terribly wrong.

«The grafftiti … it's for …» she began to explain.

«I don't want to know,» Nico said angrily. «I really, really don't want to know.»

He turned around and stormed off before Kimmy could say another word.

Chapter Eighteen – ***Das erste Spiel***

«For a kicker like you, one week of training is enough», hatte der Coach gesagt, als Nico sich nach einem der anstrengenden Trainings vorsichtig erkundigt hatte, ob er wirklich schon beim nächsten wichtigen Match dabei sein sollte. Schließlich waren ihm noch nicht mal alle Regeln des ziemlich komplizierten Spiels klar! Allerdings hatte er schnell gelernt, dass er als Kicker an den meisten Spielzügen sowieso nicht beteiligt war, dass es wirklich einzig und allein auf seine Fähigkeit ankam, den Ball in bestimmten Momenten weit und hart und gezielt zu schießen. Und das hatte Nico wirklich drauf. «It's true, you've only been a football player for a week», hatte der Coach noch hinzugefügt, «but you've been a kicker all your life.»

Mehr Zuspruch hatte Nico nicht gebraucht: Stolz und voller Vorfreude hatte er seinem ersten Match mit dem Football-Team entgegengesehen.

Am Freitagabend war es so weit. Massen von Menschen drängten auf die Ränge des Football-Feldes. Nico war schon jetzt begeistert: So viele Zuschauer hatte es bei keinem seiner Fußballspiele in Deutschland gegeben! Das gegnerische Team waren heute die Raleigh Wildcats. Raleigh war ebenfalls eine Stadt in North Carolina. Obwohl der Ort bestimmt drei Stunden von Charlotte entfernt war, hatten auch die Wildcats jede Menge Fans mitgebracht, die ihr Team jetzt schon lautstark anfeuerten. Sicher waren daran die Cheerleader nicht ganz unschuldig, die zu lauter Musik direkt vor den Zuschauern tanzten und einige der in Nicos Augen unglaublich waghalsigen Kunststücke vollführten. Gerade sah er wieder, wie Ashley durch die Luft gewirbelt wurde. Er hielt den Atem an – doch sie landete wie immer sicher und mit einem strahlenden Lächeln auf ihren Füßen.

«Patriots! Let's go!», rief der Coach in diesem Moment. Nico überprüfte noch einmal den Sitz seiner Schutzkleidung. Dann klemmte er sich den Helm unter den Arm und lief – unter dem donnernden Applaus des Publikums – mit den anderen Footballern aufs Feld. Das Spiel konnte beginnen.

Kimmy sat in her favorite seat, high up on the bleachers. The fans around her were going crazy, chanting and clapping along to one football song after another. The cheerleaders were on the field, showing off their great moves. It smelled like hot dogs and popcorn. As a big fan of everything that had to do with Jefferson High, Kimmy usually loved the big sports games, but today, she would have much rather stayed home. She was dog-tired from all the work for the campaign and from all the homework. And she was sad and confused about what had happened with Nico. In short, she was in no mood at all for big crowds or a football game. There was only one reason she was here: She was the reporter assigned to cover the match for the Express. Kimmy yawned as she took out her notepad and pen. Then she noticed that people were looking at her. Some were even waving. Kimmy looked at them. They were all girls and sophomores, but she didn't know their names. However, they clearly seemed to know who she was.

«That graffiti is so cool, Kimmy!» one girl shouted.

«So cute!» the girl next to her yelled.

«You love Jeff, we love Jeff, we love Kimmy!» another group of girls chanted cheerleader-style.

Kimmy waved back at the girls and smiled. It seemed like Ashely's idea was really working!

A minute later, the football players ran onto the field. The Jefferson Patriots' uniform was red, white and blue, like the American flag. The Raleigh Wildcats looked very impressive in black and silver. Both teams stood still to hear the American national anthem. All the fans stood up, too. Then, the game began.

The two captains of each team met in the center of the field with the two referees for the opening coin-toss. The referees were wearing their black-and-white striped uniforms. One of them was wearing a microphone. When the coin had flown in the air, everyone was quiet as the referee started to speak. His voice echoed over the field.

«The Raleigh Wildcats may choose if they want to kick first.» Then the referee continued, «Raleigh has chosen to not kick first! Gentlemen, please take your starting positions on the field with the rest of your team!»

As the crowd cheered, Kimmy made a decision. She got up from her usual seat and made her way down to the field. She wanted to get as close as she could to the sidelines to try and listen in on the coach and the team as they planned their game.

«OK, you're up, Nico!», rief der Trainer, nachdem das Team aus Raleigh entschieden hatte, den ersten Schuss an die Jefferson Patriots zu geben. «Go out there and show me that I made the right decision!»

Nico sah den Trainer überrascht an. Damit, dass er als Allererster aufs Spielfeld sollte, hatte er nicht gerechnet. «Now?», fragte er zögerlich und wandte sich dann an to Zach, «Aren't you coming, too?»

«Oh, no, no! It's all you, Nico!», hörte Nico Zach lachen. Er legte seine Hand beruhigend auf seine gepanzerten Schultern. «Don't worry, man. I've seen you kick. Just go out there and knock the hell out of that ball. Kick it as hard as you can, and the team will do the rest.»

Nico blieb nichts anderes übrig, als zu nicken. Er holte tief Luft und zog seinen Helm über. Jetzt fühlte er sich schon etwas sicherer. Zumindest konnten die vielen Fans, die jede seiner Bewegungen verfolgen würden, nicht von seinem Gesichtsausdruck ablesen, wie angespannt er gerade war.

«Nico, RUN! Show some fight!», hörte er den Coach rufen. Er rannte auf das Spielfeld und positionierte sich vor dem Ball, der schon für ihn bereitlag. Jetzt wusste er, was zu tun war. Er guckte kurz nach rechts und links, dann wieder auf den Ball. Wie aus weiter Ferne hörte er ein «Ooooooooooh» von den Fans auf den Rängen. Der langgezogene Ton wurde immer lauter, während Nico hoch konzentriert auf den Ball zusprintete.

«OoooooooooooWOW!» The loud «WOW!» came right at the end, right as Nico's foot met the ball. It flew into the air. Then there was silence.

Everyone was looking up.

«Wow!» Kimmy heard someone say, and then a second later, «Nice kick!» from someone else.

The ball hung and spun in the sky like a confused bird. Everyone started to cheer again as it came back down to the ground on the other side of the field. The Raleigh Wildcats caught it and started to run back down the field in Nico's direction, but the runner was quickly tackled by other Jefferson players. The fans went crazy again as the Wildcats' runner fell to the ground.

«Nico, come back! That's it!» Kimmy heard the coach yell. She watched Nico run back to the sideline. She moved a little closer to where he was now standing with Zach.

«Was that OK?» Nico asked.

«Man, that was awesome. Just keep doing it like that and we should be OK!» Zach answered.

When he took his helmet off, Kimmy saw that Nico looked relieved.

The game continued. One team passed and ran the football down one side, and the other passed and ran it back. After the first quarter, both teams scored touchdowns. The score was 7 : 7. Then, there was a halftime break. Kimmy didn't have time to watch the cheerleaders do their halftime show: Like a true reporter, she took her pen and notepad and wrote down everything she had seen and heard.

Nach der Halbzeitpause stürmte Nico mit den anderen zurück zum Feld. Die Spieler ließen sich schon jetzt von ihren Fans umjubeln, winkten ins Publikum und schlugen sich siegessicher auf die Brust. Über den Lautsprecher kam die Ansage: «Raleigh Wildcats will now kick the ball to Jefferson to open the second half of the game.»

Kein Einsatz für mich, dachte Nico und beobachtete gespannt, wie der Kicker der Gegner vorgehen würde. Sein Schuss konnte nicht mit Nicos mithalten: Der Ball flog so nah am Boden, dass einer der Jefferson Patriots ihn sofort abfing. Nico sah, dass es Zach war, der da mit dem Ball unter dem Arm das halbe Feld überquert hatte, bevor die Wildcats überhaupt bemerkt hatten, was passiert war.

«GO JEFF PATRIOTS! GO ZACH!», hörte Nico die Zuschauer rufen. «GO! GO! GO!»

Geschickt durchbrach Zach gleich zwei Blocks der Wildcats, rannte weiter und hechtete mitsamt Ball über die Endlinie des Spielfeldes.

«TOUCHDOWN!!!», rief der Schiedsrichter.

The referee held both his arms straight up and blew his whistle to signal that the Patriots had just won six more points. Kimmy looked up and saw the crowd dancing and jumping up and down in celebration. It was only the beginning of the second half, and Jefferson High had already made a touchdown. The score was now 13 to 7. Nico then ran out onto the field and kicked the ‹extra point› easily, making the score 14 to 7.

The game went on. The Patriots played well, but so did the Wildcats. There were some good moves and some that could have gone much better. Kimmy heard the crowd sigh and then cheer again.

Kimmy looked at her watch. There were only five more minutes to play and the score was 14 for the Patriots, 13 for the Wildcats. The players on the field all seemed a little bit tired. Then, Zach made a big mistake. As he tried to jump around a tackler, he dropped the ball, and it fell right into the hands of a Raleigh Wildcat. Kimmy and all the Patriots fans were shocked: The Raleigh Wildcats had the ball – and they were close to the goal! The Wildcats' player tried to make a touchdown, but the Jefferson's defense players tackled him at the last second.

Kimmy knew the situation was critical for both teams. Both coaches seemed to be thinking hard. Then, the Wildcats made their next move: they brought out their kicker again.

«Oh, oh,» Kimmy heard a Jefferson Patriots fan say. «If the Wildcats make this goal, they'll win! There are only two minutes left now!»

«Don't worry,» said another person, «that kicker from Raleigh hasn't been very good today. He won't make it!»

A second later, he was proven wrong. The Wildcats kicker easily made the field goal and scored three points for the team from Raleigh. Kimmy looked up at the score-board. It now read 14–16.

Oh no, she thought. She really didn't want to have to write a story about Jefferson losing their big game against Raleigh.

Nico blickte gebannt auf das Feld. Es war einfach unglaublich, wie spannend dieses Spiel war! Allerdings ging es im Moment für die Patriots nicht mehr voran, und der Trainer wirkte richtig ärgerlich: Gestikulierend und schreiend stand er am Spielfeldrand. Der Schiedsrichter pfiff, das Spiel stoppte. Jetzt blieben nur noch zwanzig Sekunden, um das Match zu entscheiden.

«We have one more chance to score before the time runs out», sagte der Coach angespannt, als er seine Mannschaft um sich versammelt hatte. «We can't risk trying for a touchdown now. We're going to have to try for a field goal. NICO!»

Nico zuckte zusammen.

«Listen», sagte der Coach und legte den Arm um seine Schultern. «I know those goalposts are far away, but I want you to try your best to get the ball in there.»

Nico blickte über das Spielfeld. Das riesige Tor war wirklich extrem weit entfernt von dem Punkt, von dem er schießen sollte. Wie ein Elfmeterschießen ist das hier, schoss es Nico durch den Kopf. Mit dem winzigen Unterschied, dass es hier eher gut 40 Meter waren, die er überwinden musste!

«It's hard, but I believe in you. If you can make it, you'll be a hero around here! Just get out there and do your best.» Mit diesen Worten gab der Trainer ihm einen Klaps auf den Rücken.

Wieder zurrte Nico seinen Helm fest. Wieder atmete er tief durch. Er lief aufs Feld, wo Zach den Ball schon für ihn bereitgelegt hatte. Jetzt kam es darauf an. Wenn er diesen Ball versenkte, hatten die Jefferson Patriots gewonnen. Was aber – Nico lief ein kalter Schauer über den Rücken –, wenn er den Ball falsch traf und das Tor meilenweit verfehlte? Reiß dich zusammen!, rief Nico sich selbst zur Ordnung. Er dachte an die vielen, vielen Stunden, die er mit einem Ball vorm Fuß zugebracht hatte. Er dachte an die zahllosen Spiele, bei denen er für seine Fußballmannschaft in Deutschland ein Spiel durch einen perfekten Elfmeterschuss entschieden hatte.

Der Schiedsrichter pfiff.

«Go!», rief der Trainer.

Kimmy held her breath. Everyone in the audience had gone silent. They were all staring at Nico. Kimmy saw Nico run towards the ball and really, really slam it. She saw that he almost fell over from swinging his body so hard, then, as he regained his balance, she – and everyone else at the game – watched the ball fly through the air. It curved a little, a little too much, and headed for the side of the goal-posts.

«Oh no! He's missing it!» Someone behind Kimmy screamed.

The ball started to fall, curving towards the goal, towards the left side.

Some fans covered their faces.

The ball hit the side of the goal-post.

Kimmy almost couldn't look at it. This was just too exciting!

The ball bounced and hit the bottom of the goal.

Then, in what seemed to Kimmy like slow motion, the ball finally fell to the ground, on the other side – the good side – of the goal.

The referees held their hands up and blew the whistles.

«It's GOOD!!!»

«Nico won the game for us!»

The fans jumped out of their seats. The Jefferson Patriots had won! They had beaten the Raleigh Wildcats 17:16! What a fantastic game!

Kimmy, who had jumped up and clapped with everybody else, quickly scribbled the last words onto her notepad. Then, while everybody else was still applauding, she found her way through the crowd and down the stairs. She wanted to get to the quiet of the Express office before everybody else started leaving. Kimmy knew it was late in the evening, but she really had to finish the article tonight. Too much work was awaiting her the next day. Plus, she had already thought of a great headline …

Kapitel neunzehn – ***Where is Sweetness?***

Nach dem Spiel herrschte eine Bombenstimmung in der Mannschaftskabine. Viele Spieler kletterten auf die Bänke, legten sich gegenseitig die Arme um die Schultern und hüpften übermütig auf und ab. Die anderen feuerten sie mit Sprechchören an, und irgendjemand hatte eine Stereoanlage auf volle Lautstärke gedreht. Zach war gerade dabei, den großen Behälter voller Eis in den Raum zu schleppen, in dem am Spielfeldrand das Trinkwasser für die Spieler gekühlt worden war. Nico hatte keine Ahnung, was er damit vorhatte, aber für den Moment kümmerte es ihn auch nicht. Er klatschte erst einmal seine Teamkollegen ab.

«Come up!», rief einer von denen, die auf der Bank standen. «You really kicked it out there, man!»

Nico lachte und sprang mit einem Satz auf die Bank. Es war wirklich ein tolles Gefühl, mitten unter diesen Jungs zu sein und auch noch von ihnen gefeiert und bejubelt zu werden.

In diesem Moment kam der Trainer zur Tür herein. Er öffnete seinen Mund, um etwas zu rufen, doch in der Sekunde schoss Zach, der mit dem vollen Behälter hinter der Tür gelauert hatte, hervor und verpasste dem Coach eine eiskalte Dusche. Der schrie auf und lachte, versuchte Zach zu packen. Doch der entwischte und wurde jetzt vom Coach durch die Umkleidekabine gejagt. Das ganze Team grölte vor Begeisterung.

Als alle sich wieder etwas beruhigt hatten, kam der Trainer auf Nico zu, hob seine Hand und sagte «High five, man!». Sie schlugen ein. «You did a great job!»

«Thank you, Coach», erwiderte Nico und grinste übers ganze Gesicht. Er hatte das Gefühl, vor Freude und Stolz fast zu platzen! Genau so hatte er sich sein neues Leben in Amerika vorgestellt. Wenn man mal davon absah, dass die Form des Balles, um den sich alles drehte, sich etwas geändert hatte! Er konnte es kaum erwarten, seinem Fußballtrainer in Deutschland von diesem aufregenden Tag zu berichten. Seine Mannschaft würde Augen machen: Nico, der American-Football-Kicker! Mr McMannon war sicher auch total stolz auf ihn. Und was würde wohl Kimmy sagen?

Bei dem letzten Gedanken zuckte er zusammen. Wieso um alles in der Welt denke ich ausgerechnet jetzt an Kimmy? dachte er ein wenig trotzig. Doch er hatte keine Zeit, weiter zu grübeln, denn etwas anderes ließ ihn aufhorchen.

«Where is Walter Payton?», fragte Zach gerade verdutzt seinen Trainer. «Seriously, where is my man, Sweetness?»

Sein Blick wanderte dabei über die frisch gestrichenen Wände des Mannschaftsraums. Dort hingen allerlei Poster und Fotos von berühmten Footballspielern und allen Teams, die es an der Jefferson High School jemals gegeben hatte. Zach würdigte sie allerdings keines Blickes.

«I don't know …», antwortete der und sah sich nun auch ratlos um.

«We must have stored him somewhere when the place got renovated», mischte sich ein anderer Spieler ein. «I haven't seen him since.»

«Walter Payton, or Sweetness, was a hall-of-fame player», erklärte der Coach an Nico gewandt. «We have a life-sized cardboard cut-out of him but now we don't know where …»

«Wait!», unterbrach Nico den Trainer. «I know where Walter Payton is!»

«What? Really? Where?», fragte Zach überrascht.

«He's in the Express office!», erklärte Nico überzeugt.

«Why would he be in there? And how do *you* know that?», fragte ein anderer Spieler skeptisch.

«I know because I *saw* the Walter Payton cut-out there. I spent a lot of time at the Express office when I worked for Kim … ähmmm … you know, the campaign …», nuschelte Nico hastig zu Ende. Er wollte wirklich nicht über Kimmy nachdenken und schon gar nicht über sie reden!

«Nico's right. I carried the cut-out there myself, but I totally forgot all about it!», mischte sich der Trainer wieder ins Gespäch ein. «What would we do without you, Nico?»

Zach nickte zustimmend. «Seems like you've become the most important member of the team, man!», lachte er.

Nico lief rot an vor lauter Stolz. Er, Nico, war ein unverzichtbarer Teil der Football-Mannschaft! Um noch ein wenig mehr Eindruck bei den anderen zu hinterlassen, bot er an: «I have an idea. I can run to the Express office right now and get the cut-out.» Um diese Uhrzeit war sicherlich keine Menschenseele mehr im Schulgebäude. Er könnte den Pappaufsteller aus dem Express-Büro holen, bevor es dort morgen früh wieder von Cheerleadern und anderen Wahlkampfhelferinnen wimmelte. Und bevor Kimmy dort wieder an ihrem Schreibtisch saß, fügte er in Gedanken hinzu.

«Yeah, we want Sweetness back now!», rief einer der Spieler.

«Totally, man!», rief Zach und klatschte Nico ab.

«It's 10.45 already, you guys should all be on your way home», sagte der Trainer weniger begeistert.

«I can go, I'll be quick», bot Nico nochmal an.

«Really quick, though», warnte der Trainer. «All the school buildings are closed at 11. Do you want someone to go with you?»

«No, no, I can go alone. It's really no problem», winkte Nico ab. Er wusste schließlich genau, wo der Pappaufsteller stand. «It'll only take me a minute.»

«OK then», sagte der Coach und lachte. «It'll be good to have Walter Payton back! Nico, get going! Everybody else, pack up and go home!»

Nico nickte in bester Laune, verließ den Mannschaftsraum und rannte allein über die dunklen Sportfelder in Richtung Schulgebäude.

At that moment in the Express office, Kimmy was yawning loudly. She had been working on her article for the past hour and it was turning out to be pretty good. It was only that last paragraph that she still didn't like. She had been changing it around again and again. Her eyes hurt and she had a hard time focusing on the words on the computer screen. She really had to finish this article tonight! Suddenly, there was a knock on the door.

«Come in,» Kimmy answered without thinking.

The door swung open and the janitor peeked his head into the office.

«Hey, young lady. Finish up in there. I've got to lock up the school doors in 10 minutes.» He said in a friendly but definite tone of voice.

«Oh, is it that late already?» Kimmy asked.

«Sure is,» he replied. «Get a move on, girl. You are the last person in the whole building. And I want to go home now myself.»

«Sure,» Kimmy nodded. «I'll be gone in a minute. Don't worry about me.»

«Alright,» the janitor mumbled. «Good night then.» He closed the door.

Kimmy sighed and stared at her last sentence again. Then, she had an idea. She deleted a few words and typed something new. Yes! Now it was perfect. Kimmy hit ‹save› and ‹print› on the keyboard. The printer came to life. Kimmy closed her document and waited for the printer to spit out her text.

At that moment, Kimmy heard someone open the door.

«I'm done, I'm leaving,» Kimmy said quickly because she thought the janitor was checking on her again.

But to her surprise it wasn't the janitor who was standing in the door. Instead, she saw the last person on earth Kimmy would have expected: Nico. He looked shocked – as if he had expected the office to be empty.

«Hey,» he said quietly and stopped in the middle of the room. «I thought that nobody would be here.»

«Hey,» she answered and looked at the floor.

Then, there was a long awkward silence.

«You played a good game,» Kimmy offered after a while.

«I'm only here to get the Walter Payton cut-out,» Nico said as if he hadn't heard her.

«Oh,» Kimmy responded, unsure what to say or do.

«Why don't you concentrate on your work,» Nico said in what sounded to Kimmy like a really cold voice. «I'll be OK.»

«Why are you so mean?» Kimmy exploded. «I should be angry, not you!»

«Really?» Nico asked cooly.

«Yes! You suddenly dropped out of my campaigning team, remember? And you didn't have the guts to tell me yourself!» Kimmy was really angry.

«That's not true!» Nico shouted back. «Why did you cancel on me on Saturday, anyway? That was your fault, not mine!»

«That has nothing to do with what I just said.» Kimmy glared at him. «Before you started playing football I was good enough for you. But now you don't even talk to me anymore!»

«And I have a good reason!» Nico answered heatedly.

«Oh, well, OK then,» Kimmy said sarcastically, «and what would that good reason be?»

«Jeff!» Nico shouted. «Stupid Jeff!»

«What?» Kimmy asked, more surprised than angry now. «What are you trying to say?»

«I don't care about your stupid Jeff, not one bit!»

«What is your problem?» Kimmy looked really hurt now. «I thought you liked it here, I thought you liked Jeff!»

«Ha!» Nico laughed bitterly. «Why would I like Jeff? I don't even know Jeff! I don't care about your stupid boyfriend!»

«What?!?» Kimmy asked again, completely flabbergasted.

«I'm talking about you and your boyfriend. I know, you're *sooooo* in love. The whole school knows!» Nico didn't hold back any of his anger as he spoke. In a mocking high pitched girly voice he said, «Kimmy loves Jeff, Jeff loves Kimmy.» Then he added, almost shouting again, «Your love graffiti was pretty hard to miss!»

Suddenly, Kimmy understood. For a second, she only stared at Nico, who still looked extremely angry.

Then she opened her mouth to answer, but she didn't get a chance to speak: With a loud KKKKKRRRRRRRKKKK, the office door locked, and all the lights went out.

Chapter Twenty –
Eine lange dunkle Nacht, Teil 1

Nico zuckte zusammen. Es war stockfinster. Er konnte Kimmy nicht sehen, aber dem Geräusch nach war sie von ihrem Stuhl aufgesprungen. Sie war stumm vor Schreck.

Nico war der Erste, der wieder sprach: «What is going on?»

«Do you have a watch? With a light?», fragte Kimmy tonlos.

«No, but – my cell phone has a clock.» Er angelte das Telefon aus seiner Tasche. «It's eleven», sagte er.

«Oh, no,» Kimmy klang vollkommen fassungslos. «I *can't* believe it. This did *not* just happen.»

«What happened?», wiederholte Nico. Seine Augen hatten sich noch immer nicht an die Dunkelheit gewöhnt. Auch das schwache Licht seines Handys konnte nicht viel ausrichten.

«All the doors lock down automatically at 11 o'clock every night», sagte Kimmy matt. «The janitor – he even told me to leave. There's no way out of here until he comes back in the morning.»

«Let's call your parents! Or the McMannons», sagte Nico zuversichtlich. «They can call the janitor and …»

«There's no reception down here», seufzte Kimmy.

Nico blickte auf sein Handy. Tatsächlich: kein Empfang.

«What about the internet? We can send someone a message!», hatte Nico noch eine Idee.

«All electricity turns off, too. To save energy, I guess.» Sie lachte bitter.

Jetzt erst bemerkte Nico, dass das Summen der Computer tatsächlich verstummt war.

«Maybe we can climb out of a window?» Langsam gingen auch Nico die Vorschläge aus.

«We're in the basement», seufzte Kimmy. «No windows.»

«Oh, no», sagte jetzt auch Nico. Ihre Lage war wirklich aussichtslos. Ein paar Augenblicke stand er einfach nur still da. Langsam konnte er schemenhaft Gegenstände im dunklen Raum erkennen. Er tastete sich in Richtung von Kimmy. Dann ließ er sich vorsichtig auf einen Stuhl fallen, der direkt neben ihrem Schreibtisch stand. Von hier aus konnte er sehen, dass Kimmy immer noch dastand wie vom Donner gerührt.

Kimmy could not believe it. She stared into the dark, unwilling to accept the fact that they were really locked in. This was the stupidest, most frustrating thing that could have happened!

«Why don't you sit down,» she heard Nico's voice.

She automatically plopped down onto her desk chair.

«My parents!» she said nervously, «they're going to absolutely freak out when I don't come home tonight.»

Nico didn't respond right away.

«The McMannons will be worried, too,» he said quietly.

Then they didn't say anything for a while.

Kimmy's mind was racing. She took a deep breath. Calm

down, she told herself, there is nothing we can do to change the situation. This is it. We're going to be here all night. We're going to have to make the best out of it. She took another deep breath. Calm down, she told herself again, relax.

«OK,» she said, feeling a little bit better already, «let's be practical here.»

Despite the darkness, she could now see that Nico was looking at her.

«We're locked in. There is nothing we can do. Let's try to make the best out of a bad situation.»

«OK,» was Nico's only answer.

«We have drinks here and lots of cookies. We won't be hungry or thirsty. I think there are a couple of blankets somewhere, from a picnic we did a little while ago. We can use them in case we get cold. And if we get tired, the couches are pretty comfortable.»

«OK,» Nico said again.

Then they didn't say anything for a little while. Kimmy could tell that her eyes where adjusting more and more to the dark. She decided to try and talk to Nico again, to make the situation a little better.

«So, as this is my office, let me be a good host.» She laughed a little. «Can I get you anything to drink? Are you hungry?»

Nico seemed to think for a few seconds.

«I am pretty thirsty,» he said. «And … I could eat!»

«Alright,» Kimmy said and stood up. «Let's move over there, to the couch. The sodas are over there. And the cookies too, I think.»

She carefully maneuvered through the room, with Nico following her closely. Then, they both sat down on the couch. Kimmy grabbed some cans from the floor.

She held them close to her face. «There's a coke for you,» she said and handed it to Nico, «and another one for me.»

«Thanks,» Nico said. She heard him pop open the can and take a long drink.

«Cookies?» she asked next. «I think these are the double chocolate ones, but I'm not sure.»

«That sounds good,» Nico said.

«Alright,» Kimmy answered, glad they had something to do. She opened the box and offered it to Nico.

For the moment, there didn't seem to be anything else to say, so they sat together, silently, in the dark, eating cookies and drinking their cokes.

Irgendwann wurde Nico die Stille zu viel. Jetzt, da er den ersten Schreck überwunden hatte, war ihm schlagartig wieder eingefallen, was in dem Moment passiert war, bevor es dunkel wurde.

Einerseits wollte er die jetzt eigentlich ganz entspannte Stimmung zwischen ihm und Kimmy nicht stören. Schließlich mussten sie wohl oder übel noch die ganze Nacht hier zusammen sitzen! Andererseits war er eben gerade noch richtig wütend auf sie gewesen! Und das ganze Thema war überhaupt noch nicht geklärt. Sollte er etwas sagen?

Zu seiner Verblüffung hörte er plötzlich seine eigene Stimme fest und ernst fragen: «So who is Jeff? How long have you been his girlfriend? Why didn't you tell me?»

Statt einer Antwort hörte er ein glucksendes Geräusch aus der Dunkelheit. Aus dem Glucksen wurde ein Kichern. Aus dem Kichern wurde ein Lachen. Kimmy lachte so sehr, dass sie fast vom Sofa rutschte. «I'm sorry, I'm sorry», japste sie. «I'm so sorry! But this is just too crazy!» Sie verschluckte sich vor Lachen und bekam einen Hustenanfall, der sie allerdings nicht davon abhielt, weiter zu kichern.

Nico starrte sie sprachlos an.

Kimmy beruhigte sich und setzte sich wieder richtig auf die Couch, diesmal allerdings Nico zugewandt. Sie wischte sich ihre Lachtränen aus den Augen und räusperte sich.

«Nico», sagte sie mit etwas ernsthafterer Stimme. «Jeff is not a boy. Jeff is short for Jefferson! People call our school Jeff High all the time!»

Jetzt war es Nico, der wie vom Donner gerührt dasaß.

«The graffiti is not from a boy», sprach Kimmy weiter. «Ashley made it! She wanted to do something really special for ...»

«... *your campaign!*», beendete Nico ihren Satz und schlug sich mit der Hand vor die Stirn. Jeff und Jefferson, dachte er, das ist doch wohl das Naheliegendste der Welt! Warum bin ich darauf nicht gekommen? Es ist wirklich unglaublich, dachte er als Nächstes: Ich bin eifersüchtig auf eine Wahlwerbung und zu doof, es von selbst zu bemerken!

«Exactly!», sagte Kimmy und fing schon wieder an zu lachen. «I'm so sorry I laughed. You sounded so serious, and I had been wondering what was wrong, too, but it was just too funny!»

Nico war das Ganze immer noch zu peinlich, um einfach mitzulachen. Ich bin so ein Vollidiot, dachte er.

«It was just a misunderstanding», sagte Kimmy und rückte noch etwas näher an ihn heran. «And I'm sorry it happened.»

«Me too», grummelte Nico und schämte sich immer noch ein bisschen. Dass Kimmys Knie plötzlich seins berührte, bemerkte er allerdings trotzdem sofort.

Kapitel einundzwanzig – **A long dark night, part 2**

For once, Kimmy was thankful for the darkness. «There is no other boy I like, Nico,» she said softly.

Nico, who had turned towards her, looked her straight in the eyes. «No … *other* … boy?» he asked slowly and carefully, as if he didn't trust his own ears.

«I like you,» Kimmy whispered. She could feel her pulse racing. Then, for a split second, it felt as if her heart skipped a beat: Nico had put his arm around her.

«I like you too,» he said.

Kimmy rested her head on his shoulder.

They sat together comfortably for a little while.

«Sorry I had to cancel our date,» Kimmy whispered after a while.

«Why did you cancel it?» Nico asked.

«I had a date with Jeff.» She laughed out loud. This time, Nico laughed, too.

«I had too much work,» she said, «that was all. I really had no choice.»

Kimmy could feel that Nico nodded his head. He believed her.

«And …» Nico spoke again, «what did you and Ashley whisper about at that one campaign meeting? When Ashley said it was a secret?»

«You,» Kimmy said simply and turned her head to face Nico.

«Oh,» Nico said and pulled Kimmy even closer.

Kimmy closed her eyes, and they kissed. Then, they kissed again. Kimmy's heart was still beating much too quickly, and she had a strange, fluttery feeling in her stomach. It felt wonderful.

Nico konnte sein Glück noch gar nicht begreifen. Sein Herz schlug viel schneller als sonst, und in seinem Bauch tanzten die Schmetterlinge. Irgendwann hatte Kimmy eine Decke unter dem Sofa hervorgeangelt, über sich und Nico ausgebreitet und sich wieder in seinen Arm gekuschelt. So gut wie jetzt gerade hatte Nico sich noch nie in seinem Leben gefühlt.

«Can I ask you something?», fragte Kimmy in diesem Moment.

«Sure», antwortete er.

«Did you *only* join my campaign team because you couldn't play soccer?», fragte sie.

«Mmmh, let me think», antwortete Nico gut gelaunt. «Yes, it was only because I couldn't play soccer. Why else?» Er grinste.

Kimmy sah ihn gespielt beleidigt an.

«OK,» lachte er. «I also joined your campaign because I liked you» – er küsste sie wieder – «because I wanted to be near you.»

«Good», lächelte Kimmy zurück.

Jetzt war auch Nico eine Frage eingefallen. Keine besonders wichtige, aber die Antwort darauf wollte er schon gerne hören.

«Can I ask you something?», fragte er genau so wie zuvor Kimmy.

«Sure!», sagte sie.

«How on earth did you and Ashley get the principal to agree to graffiti on the school wall?»

Kimmy laughed. «It looks like normal spray-paint, but it's not. The color washes right off. One rain storm, no more graffiti.»

«No more Kimmy loves Jeff», lachte Nico mit ihr.

«Only Kimmy and Nico from now on», antwortete sie, und Nicos Herz schlug gleich wieder Purzelbäume.

«Hey, there's something I want you to see,» Kimmy said excitedly after they had been all snuggled up on the couch for an hour or so.

She lifted the blanket, felt her way over to her desk and came back with a piece of paper.

«My article! On the football match!» she said proudly. «D'you want to read it?»

Nico took out his cell phone again and by the dim light of its display, he began to read.

«Wow!» he said right away.

«Do you like it?» Kimmy said, excited.

«How could I not like it?» Nico laughed. «The headline is: ‹New kicker new star!›»

«And I wrote that *before* I kissed you,» Kimmy said, grinning.

«Thanks!» Nico said and kissed her on her nose.

Then he looked at the article again. «Wow,» he said when he had finished. «This is so good! You are such a good writer!»

«Thank you,» Kimmy said happily.

«Did I ever tell you that my mom is a journalist?» Nico asked.

«Really? Cool!» Kimmy exclaimed.

«I think she would be really impressed, too! You write like you are ...» Kimmy could tell that he was looking for the right word in English.

«... like you are not a student! Like it is your real job!»

«... like a professional!» Kimmy said, beaming with pride at his compliment.

«Yes! Like a pro!» Nico said. «I learned that word from Mr McMannon on my first day here!»

«I do want to be a professional journalist,» she said. «I'm really serious about that.»

Suddenly, she noticed a change in Nico's face. «Are you,» he began, «are you also serious … about us?» he asked slowly.

«Yes!» she said as she put down the printout and curled up in his arms again. «It might be hard sometimes to find time. I'm still, way, way, too busy: Homework, the campaign and your football practice! But I can't think of anything better,» she looked up at him, «than to be … your girlfriend.»

Kimmy could see from his smile that he couldn't imagine anything better either.

«I think I know what we can do about that problem,» Nico grinned. «We will have to find a new time to meet, but I want to help you with your campaign again. I want to help you win the class presidency.»

«Yey!» Kimmy said, excitedly. «Thanks, Nico!»

And then, after some long talks about new campaign ideas and a whole lot of kissing, Kimmy and Nico finally fell asleep.

Chapter Twenty-two – ***Alle! Zusammen!***

Am nächsten Morgen wurde Nico unsanft aus dem Schlaf gerissen.

«They're here!», rief eine laute Männerstimme im gleichen

Moment, in dem plötzlich grelles Licht den Raum flutete. «I found them, they're fine!»

Verdutzt sah Nico sich um. Es dauerte einige Sekunden, bis er sich orientieren konnte. Ein Sofa, das Express-Büro …

«They're here!», rief der Mann, der da im Türrahmen stand, noch einmal laut auf den Gang hinaus.

Jetzt war ihm alles wieder klar. Er sprang vom Sofa auf. Auch Kimmy saß jetzt kerzengerade. Nico konnte ihr gerade noch zulächeln, da war der Raum, der so lange so still gewesen war, plötzlich voller Menschen.

«My baby, my darling!», rief eine Frau und schloss Kimmy in ihre Arme. Ein Mann, dem anzusehen war, dass er die ganze Nacht keine Auge zugemacht hatte, tat es ihr gleich. Beide sahen überglücklich aus. Das waren dann wohl Kimmys Eltern, dachte Nico noch, da stürzte auch schon jemand auf ihn zu.

«Nico, honey, oh, thank heaven!» Es war Mrs McMannon, die ihn umarmte. «We were so worried!»

Mr McMannon klopfte ihm als Nächstes auf die Schulter. Auch er sah aus, als wäre eine große Last von ihm gefallen.

Zu seiner großen Überraschung waren das noch längst nicht alle Leute. Der Mann, der als Erstes reingekommen war, schloss Nico, musste wohl der Hausmeister sein. Da standen auch noch Zach und Ashley, der Schuldirektor, der Football Coach, zahlreiche Cheerleader und die halbe Footballmannschaft … alle schienen die ganze Nacht auf den Beinen gewesen zu sein, um ihn und Kimmy zu suchen. Nico fiel sofort auf, dass einige der Footballer sogar noch die Trainingsklamotten anhatten, die sie gestern bei der kleinen Siegesfeier getragen hatten. Alle sahen müde, aber sehr erleichtert aus.

Kimmy looked around the room. So many people were here! Her mom and dad, the McMannons, her friends from the cheerleading squad, some of the football players and, of course, Nico. After the night in the dark, quiet office, it was so nice to hear so many voices and to see so many smiling faces. Everybody had been looking for her and Nico, everybody had worked together to find them. Kimmy saw her mom and dad hug each other and then Mr and Mrs McMannon, with big smiles on their faces. The cheerleaders and football players were all talking and laughing. Kimmy couldn't believe her eyes when she saw that even Zach and Ashley were high-fiving each other. Everybody seemed more than happy to finally have found the two missing people.

«Hey Nico,» Zach shouted across the room, «I'll take care of Walter Payton for you!»

Kimmy saw Nico laugh. «I had totally forgotten about him,» he said as he watched Zach shoulder the life-sized cardboard cut-out of his idol.

«Let's all go upstairs,» Kimmy heard Principal Monroe say at the same moment. She had never seen him look so relieved.

«Yeah, let's get Kimmy and Nico out of this basement,» somebody else laughed.

«I'm sure the two would enjoy some fresh air and sun light!» another voice added.

Kimmy couldn't agree more. As she climbed up the stairs, she could still hear everybody talk and laugh. The boys and girls were chatting and smiling, and so were all the men and women.

«So glad Kimmy and Nico are OK,» she heard one of the cheerleaders say.

«So glad we finally found them,» a football player added.

Kimmy smiled to herself. It was so great to be around all these nice people again!

Als er in die Sonne trat, die in Charlotte auch schon früh am Morgen vom Himmel strahlte, fühlte Nico sich wie neugeboren. So unglaublich die Ereignisse der letzten Nacht gewesen waren, jetzt war er erst mal froh, wieder Licht, Luft und Leute um sich zu haben. Wo war eigentlich Kimmy? Er entdeckte sie neben Zach und Ashley, die beide gespannt zuhörten, was Kimmy ihnen zu berichten hatte. Richtig ungewohnt war es, dachte Nico, die beiden so einträchtig zu sehen! Kimmy hatte ihre Schilderung anscheinend beendet, denn sie sah sich suchend um und lief, als sie Nico entdeckte, in ein paar schnellen Schritten auf ihn zu.

«There you are», sagte sie und stupste ihn an.

«Hey», grinste Nico.

«What a night!», lächelte sie und blinzelte in die Sonne. «It's good to see the sun, though.»

«Yes!» Nico nickte. «And it's so nice to see all these people!»

«All these happy people», verbesserte Kimmy ihn lachend.

«Did you see, even Zach and Ashley are smiling at each other!»

«Unbelievable!», grinste Nico.

«We should lock ourselves into the Express office more often», grinste sie.

«All the cheerleaders and football players seem to be best friends now», bemerkte Nico.

Beide beobachteten das Lachen und die Gespräche der anderen. Auf einmal hatte Nico eine Idee. Auch Kimmy guckte plötzlich ganz aufgeregt.

«We should use this for my campaign!», rief sie

«Yes!», antwortete Nico. Anscheinend hatten sie gerade die gleiche Idee.

«Ashley wanted me to do a campaign only for girls, but I don't want to do that – I want to be class president for everyone!», sprudelte Kimmy.

«Are you thinking what I'm thinking?», fragte Nico.

«Let's talk to the cheerleaders – *and* to the football team!», sagte Kimmy und zog ihn an der Hand mit sich.

It didn't take much convincing. After about five minutes, the football players were on board.

«Kimmy for president!» one boy yelled.

«Kimmy, Kimmy, we love Kimmy!» some other players shouted, cheerleader-style, before cracking up with laughter.

«Seriously,» Zach added, still balancing the Walter Payton cut-out, «we'll help you.»

Even Ashley liked the idea. «My graffiti was fantastic, though,» she added, «and all the girls loved it!»

«Not all the boys loved it, though,» Kimmy said and grinned at Nico. She could see that his ears turned a little pink, but he grinned back at her.

Ashley continued, «The most important thing is that you win the election! And since I'm your campaign manager, I'll do whatever it takes to make you win – boys or no boys!»

«Thanks, Ash,» Kimmy said.

«Actually,» Ashley continued, «this could be a fantastic new strategy! I mean, we cheerleaders, we're the most popular girls at the school. And the footballers are the most popuar boys. You've already had the cheerleaders behind you, and now the football team is on your side, too. I don't think that has ever happened before in Jeff High history! And I think I know just what we can do!»

Kimmy smiled at her best friend and squeezed Nico's hand. For the first time in a while, she felt like she might be able to do it: She could win the class president election! *They* could *all* win the class president election, everyone, together!

Kapitel dreiundzwanzig – **The election**

Nach der unfreiwilligen Übernachtung im Express-Büro war Nicos Leben wie auf den Kopf gestellt. Er hatte das Gefühl, dass er erst jetzt – und nicht schon vor vielen Wochen – richtig in den USA angekommen war. Jeder seiner Nachmittage war seit kurzem gefüllt, und immer war er von Freunden umgeben: Wenn er nicht gerade auf dem Sportplatz stand und seine Kicks perfektionierte, tüftelte er mit den anderen Footballern und den Mädchen in Kimmys Team an neuen Ideen für den Wahlkampf. Das alles, musste Nico zu seiner eigenen Überraschung feststellen, war fast noch besser als sein altes Leben in Deutschland! Ganz zu schweigen davon, dass Nicos Herz jedes Mal schneller schlug, wenn er in Kimmys Nähe war … Nach den holprigen Anfängen in Charlotte war es wirklich unglaublich, wie schnell sich plötzlich alles zum Besten gewendet hatte!

Tatsächlich hatte sich auch Kimmys und sein Plan, die Footballer für den Wahlkampf einzuspannen, als die beste Idee überhaupt herausgestellt: Genau wie die Cheerleader waren auch die Footballer reinste Magneten, wenn es darum ging, das Interesse der anderen Sophomores für Kimmys Kampagne zu gewinnen. Auch auf Ashleys Einfälle war nach wie vor Verlass. Nico musste grinsen, wenn er daran dachte, welchen Ansturm sie erzeugt hatten, als die Footballer sich in voller Montur für Schnappschüsse mit ihren Fans aus der zehnten Klasse bereitgestellt hatten – um gleichzeitig Flyer mit dem Aufdruck «Vote for Kimmy Williams!» zu verteilen. Natürlich war er selbst, Nico, auch dabei gewesen. Oder die Aktion, bei der die Cheerleader für alle spontan einen Auftritt in der Cafeteria hingelegt hatten – in T-Shirts, auf denen Kimmys lächelndes Gesicht prangte. Und dann noch die Wahlparty, die die Footballer und Cheerleader zusammen organisiert hatten und zu der fast der gesamte Jahrgang erschienen war!

Heute nun war endlich Kimmys großer Tag gekommen: der Tag der Wahl, der Tag der Entscheidung! Zusammen mit den anderen Sophomores hatte Nico sich in der riesigen Sporthalle eingefunden, denn hier sollte das Ergebnis der Auszählung verkündet werden. Obwohl Nico sich schon an den Gedanken gewöhnt hatte, auf eine High School zu gehen, die ungefähr viermal so groß war wie seine Schule in Deutschland, war er, während er sich in der Halle umguckte, beeindruckt von den Massen an Schülerinnen und Schülern, die alle zu seinem Jahrgang gehörten: Fast tausend Schüler hatten heute ihre Stimme abgegeben – wie viele davon hatten wohl bei Kimmys Namen ihr Kreuzchen gemacht?

It was only minutes now until the principal would walk onto the stage and announce who had won the elections, and Kimmy could not stand still. Jumping from one foot to the other and nervously curling long strands of hair with her fingers she waited with all the other 10th graders in the gym. Nico, Zach, Ashley and all her friends and campaign helpers were right by her side.

«I'm so sure we won,» Ashley kept saying, «Seriously! I'm so sure!» But, Kimmy noticed, she also looked a little stressed.

«I'm sooooooo nervous,» Kimmy said.

«When we're nervous before a game coach always says: You're not nervous, you're excited.» Zach responded. «So, be excited, Kimmy, don't be nervous!»

«Easy for you to say,» Kimmy replied and kept jumping from one foot to the other.

«Calm down.» Nico took her hand. «You're so …»

It looked like he couldn't think of the right word.

«Nervous? Worried? Terrified?» Kimmy gave him some alternatives that described the way she felt.

«You're jumping around so much,» Nico said.

«I'm jumping around,» she said and couldn't help but smile a little, «because I'm nervous, worried, terrified …»

«… and jumpy. That's what you are.» He grinned. «Jumpy!»

«OK, I'm jumpy,» she said. «You'd be jumpy if you were running for …»

«There's Principal Monroe!» Ashley cut Kimmy's sentence short. «He's going on stage. This is it!»

«Hello, sophomore class, it is wonderful to see everyone today», begann der Schulleiter seine Rede. Alle Schüler klatschten. «I don't want to keep you waiting much longer, only a few words before we hear the results of this year's class president elections.»

«He says that every time!», flüsterte Ashley und rollte mit den Augen, wie Nico es schon eine Weile nicht mehr gesehen hatte.

Auch Zach stöhnte hörbar auf, als ob er mit nichts Gutem rechnete.

«What?», wisperte Nico, doch Zach deutete nur auf die Bühne und zuckte mit den Schultern.

Nico merkte schnell, was die beiden meinten: ‹Nur ein paar Worte› waren für Principal Monroe nichts anderes als ein halbstündiger Vortrag über die Rechte und Pflichten eines Jahrgangssprechers, der so langweilig war, dass jetzt Nico begann, von einem Fuß auf den anderen zu hüpfen.

Zach und Ashley sahen abwechselnd auf ihre Armbanduhren.

Sogar Kimmy gähnte.

Dann, endlich, wurde es wieder interessant. «Let's welcome this year's candidates», rief der Schulleiter ins Mikrophon. «Devon Mahone, Kimberley Williams and Rashid Jackson!»

Nico drückte noch schnell Kimmys Hand, da war sie auch schon mit den beiden Gegenkandidaten auf dem Weg zur Bühne. Alle drei sahen ziemlich nervös aus.

Kimmy's legs were shaking as she climbed the steps to the stage. She stood next to Devon and Rashid and tried to smile into the audience.

«I'm now going to announce the results of this year's sophomore class president election,» Principal Monroe continued. «There are 1132 students in this year's sophomore class,» he explained. «1002 cast their votes.»

Kimmy felt even more nervous. She searched the audience for Nico. There he was, smiling and waving at her.

«As I said,» the principal repeated, «we counted 1002 votes.» He looked at his notes. «Out of these votes, 117 were cast for Devon Mahone.»

Kimmy saw Devon hang is head. His supporters clapped with sad faces. He lifted his head up and tried to smile like it was no big deal to him. She tried to feel sorry for Devon, but she really just felt more nervous and, as Zach had put it, more excited! As she waited for Principal Monroe to continue, she quickly did the Math in her head. I need 443 votes or more, she thought. Am I really going to win, she asked herself, or will Rashid be the next class president?

Principal Monroe also had all the numbers written down. «117 votes for Devon,» he said again, «which means that there are 885 votes left.»

Kimmy couldn't believe how slow the principal was going.

«Before I announce the new president, let me just say that the results were very clear this year.»

Kimmy nervously moved from one foot to the other.

«Out of the 885, 601 – yes, 601! – were cast for one of these two candidates,» the principal announced.

601! Wow! Kimmy thought. Her pulse was racing. Her palms were wet. Her stomach felt tingly. Was it her? Was it?

«A very impressive outcome, I say,» Principal Monroe added importantly.

Come on, come on, come on, say it!, Kimmy almost wanted to shout out loud.

«The winner of this year's sophomore class elections, the new sophomore class president, is …»

The whole gym had gone absolutely silent.

Kimmy closed her eyes.

She held her breath.

«Kimberley Williams!» Principal Monroe shouted. «Congratulations, Kimberley!»

Der Jubelsturm, der jetzt in der Sporthalle ausbrach, war unbeschreiblich. Zach, Ashley, Nico und all die anderen, die so lange für Kimmys Sieg gearbeitet hatten, fielen sich in die Arme. Am liebsten wäre Nico auf die Bühne gestürmt, aber das ging nicht: Der Schulleiter hatte schon wieder das Wort ergriffen.

«Sophomore class», sprach er die Schüler in gewichtigem Tonfall an, «I present to you: the new sophomore class president: Kimberley Williams!» Damit gab er sein Mikrophon an Kimmy weiter.

Die Zehntklässler klatschten und jubelten.

«I can't tell you how happy I am», begann Kimmy ihre Ansprache an den Jahrgang. «However, there is one thing that I do know: I wouldn't be here if it wasn't for all my friends and supporters.»

Wieder gab es tobenden Applaus.

«Thank you to my campaign team, the Jeff High cheerleading squad, and the football team!», rief sie als Nächstes.

Die Sophomores jubelten und klatschten noch lauter.

«I couldn't have done it without my campaign manager, who also happens to be the best friend a girl could ask for: Ashley McMannon! Come up here, Ashley, this is your victory, too!»

Nico sah Ashley auf die Bühne klettern. Die beiden Freundinnen umarmten sich, und Ashley winkte strahlend ins Publikum.

«Last but definitely not least, I had help from someone really special, someone who came all the way from Europe to be a Jeff High sophomore with all of us: Nico Wagner! Come join us on stage, Nico!»

Unter lautem Klatschen ging auch Nico auf die Bühne.

«Thanks, Nico», flüsterte Kimmy ihm ins Ohr, als er sie – vor den Augen des gesamten Jahrgangs – in die Arme schloss.

Chapter Twenty-four – ***Sonntags-Sundaes***

A few days after the elections, Nico and Kimmy were sitting at Kimmy's favorite café in a quiet street of downtown Charlotte. The sun was shining brightly, there was no cloud in the sky: It was an absolutely perfect Sunday afternoon, an absolutely perfect day for a romantic date.

«I'm so glad to be here with you,» Kimmy said as she tried some of her ice-cream.

«Me too.» Nico smiled. «I'm glad you weren't too busy for

me this time,» he added jokingly, reminding Kimmy of the time she had not been able to go on their very first date.

«Oh, come on,» she said, «that's ancient history!»

«True,» Nico nodded and ate a big spoonfull of ice-cream.

«Do you want to try mine?» she offered and pointed to her ice-cream. «Your strawberry sauce is great, but you should try the caramel cream on mine!»

«Sure,» Nico said and spooned some ice-cream from Kimmy's cup.

«So, which Sundae do you like better, mine or yours?» Kimmy asked.

«Hmmmh?» Nico said, looking confused. «Which Sunday?»

Kimmy, who normally thought that Nico's English was really good, had to laugh. «S-U-N-D-A-E,» she spelled the word for him. «Not the weekday. It's another word for ice-cream.»

«Oh!» Nico said. «The caramel cream is good, but I like mine better. Nothing is better than strawberries.»

«I think *you* are better than strawberries,» Kimmy said flirtly.

Nico didn't answer. Instead, he leaned over and kissed Kimmy on her nose. She giggled.

«Look at those love-birds,» somebody shouted at that moment. «Aren't they cute?»

Kimmy turned around.

«Hey Kimmy, I mean, hello, Madame President!», rief Ashley grinsend. «Hey Nico!»

«Hey guys», sagte Zach, der neben seiner Schwester stand.

«Hey», antworteten Kimmy und Nico fast wie aus einem Mund.

Nico musterte seine beiden Gastgeschwister. Es war immer noch ein ungewohnter Anblick, die beiden zusammen zu sehen, ohne dass die Fetzen flogen. Kimmy schien den gleichen Gedanken zu haben.

«So what are you two doing here, together?», fragte sie.

«You know», fing Ashley umständlich an zu erklären, «I was bored and hungry, and I ran into Zach when I went to get some food from the kitchen, and we decided to, you know, go out for something instead.»

Zach nickte.

«It's funny to see you two … do something together», sagte Kimmy offen heraus.

«Oh well», Ashley seufzte dramatisch, «he's my brother, what can I do?»

«I really only had no-one better to go with», fügte Zach mit einem Grinsen hinzu, worauf Ashley ihn in die Seite knuffte.

«OK», sagte Kimmy schnell, «before you start fighting again, why don't you sit down with us and order some ice-cream?»

Nico rückte seinen Stuhl dichter an Kimmys. Ashley und Zach angelten sich zwei freie Stühle vom Nachbartisch.

«Don't know what to order, any suggestions?», fragte Zach.

«Get the strawberry ice-cream», sagte Nico in der Sekunde, in der Kimmy antwortete: «Try the caramel sundae!»

Zach guckte sich um. «Do they have a special of the day?»

«They have the same ice-cream every day», wusste Kimmy zu berichten, «the special of the day is regular food, you know, like sandwiches or hot meals.»

«I could go for a real meal», sagte Zach. «We football players, we have to stay strong, right, Nico?»

Nico lachte, denn er hatte vorhin im Vorbeigehen eine Tafel mit den Tagesangeboten gesehen.

«What's so funny?» Kimmy asked when she saw that Nico was laughing about something.

«The special of the day,» Nico said, «it's bratwurst and potato salad! I just had to think of my last football ... I mean ... soccer game at home. My mom made bratwurst and potato salad for everyone because she said I wouldn't get any in the USA. And then, when I came here, for my first dinner in Charlotte ...»

«... Mom made bratwurst and potato salad!» Ashley finished his sentence.

«Yes,» Nico nodded, «and on my first day at school,» he turned to Kimmy, «remember what we had at the cafeteria?»

Of course Kimmy remembered. «Bratwurst and potato salad,» she answered, laughing. «I think that food is following you, Nico.»

«I know exactly what to order then,» Zach grinned, «how about you, Ashley?»

«Sure, why not. I am pretty hungry!» she answered and went inside the cafe to order with her brother.

Kimmy ate the last few spoons of her ice-cream, then she looked at Nico again.

«Did I mention that I'm really happy to be here with you?» she asked. «I'm always having such a nice time with you!»

«Yes.» Nico smiled.

«I'm really glad things turned out the way they did,» Kimmy said. «It's almost unbelievable, isn't it? I mean, you're on the football team, I'm class president, Zach and Ashley aren't fighting ...»

«And we're together!» he added to her list.

«That's the best part.» Kimmy smiled and took his hand again.

Unglaublich war das richtige Wort, fand Nico. Fast wie ein Traum war sein neues Leben in den USA. Er konnte sich kaum noch vorstellen, wie es vorher gewesen war. Vorher, als er noch nie von Charlotte gehört hatte und als er noch kein Jefferson Patriot gewesen war. Zum Glück, dachte Nico, liegt der größte Teil des halben Jahres noch vor mir! Was ihn wohl alles noch erwartete, bis es im Februar wieder nach Deutschland ging? Herbst und Winter lagen vor ihm, Weihnachtsferien und Silvester, jede Menge lange Schultage und zahllose Stunden auf dem Trainingsplatz. Was auch immer alles noch passieren wird, dachte Nico, während er in die Sonne blinzelte und Kimmys Hand in seiner hielt, eine Sache ist jetzt schon sicher: Mit Kimmy, Zach und Ashley, mit Football und den Jungs vom Team werden es unter Garantie die besten Monate meines Lebens!

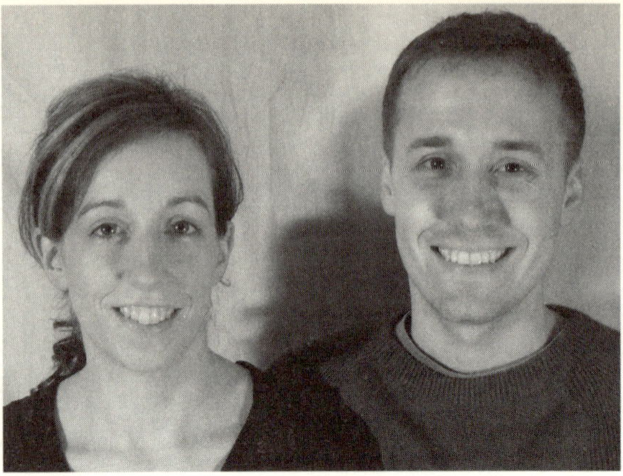

© Lisa Schüler

Stefanie Schulz, Jahrgang 1978, studierte Englisch in Göttingen und den USA, bevor sie 2003 Deutschlehrerin an einer amerikanischen Universität wurde. Dieser Job brachte sie auf die Idee, eine deutsch-englische Geschichte zu erzählen. Ihre Doktorarbeit schrieb sie über amerikanisches Theater.

Daniel Quinlan, geboren 1979 in Chicago, studierte Physik und arbeitete als Lehrer, Übersetzer und DJ in den USA und Deutschland. Seine Koautorin lernte er 2000 auf einem deutsch-amerikanischen Austausch kennen. Seit 2005 ist sein Wohnsitz Göttingen, wo er für seine Doktorarbeit Laser baut.

Bereits bei rotfuchs von ihnen erschienen:
«See you – im nächsten Sommer» (21352),
«See you again – mit Herzklopfen» (21378),
«Crazy days – und viel Theater» (21433) und
«Crazy days – und noch mehr Drama» (21496).